iHATERELIGION

MIKE JARRELL

ihatereligion
© 2011 by Mike Jarrell

All scriptures unless otherwise mentioned are from the English Standard Version. Scripture quotations marked "ESV" are taken from The Holy Bible: English Standard Version, copyright © 2001, Wheaton: Good News Publishers. Used by permission. All rights reserved.

Published by PCG Legacy, a division of Pilot Communications Group, Inc. 317 Appaloosa Trail Waco, TX 76712

ISBN: 978-1-936417-27-8

Printed in the United States of America

HOW TO ORDER:

www.ihatereligionbook.com

ACKNOWLEDGMENTS

I would like to give a special thanks to Lisa Wilson, Rob Morris, Chris Carr, and Jamie Swalm for their support in this venture. I would also like to thank my wonderful partner, Jackie, for her encouragement to write this book.

FOREWORD

I remember one Sunday after church a couple approached me and they were angry. During communion, a young woman came into the sanctuary holding a cup of coffee. The couple was angry that this young woman had "defiled" the sanctuary during communion. I desperately tried to show them how God cared more about this young woman than her cup of coffee in the sanctuary during communion. They did not get it. They ended up leaving the church.

I will never forget my first day on the job as the new Senior Pastor. While walking to the church office and passing the sanctuary, I noticed a large sign on the sanctuary door. It read, "Thou shalt not bring food or drink into the sanctuary." At that moment, I committed my first official act on my first day as the senior pastor. I tore the sign down.

This is what Mike Jarrell's book, *I Hate Religion*, is all about. Tearing down the rules of religion and replacing them with the love of God.

Every once in a while, a book comes along that clearly addresses a spiritual issue for our day and time. *I Hate Religion* is just such a book. Mike Jarrell has put his finger on one of the reasons why churches are losing people in record numbers and struggling to attract new people. It's the difference between focusing on "religion" versus focusing on a true "relationship" with God. Religion focuses on issues and rules; relationship focuses on the heart.

Mike correctly identifies that many today feel burned by the church because of performance standards based on things like how we dress, how we look, how we sing, and even how we pray. These issues are part of "religion" and not the true message of love and hope Jesus offers sinners in "relationship" with Him. As Mike says, no one gets any style points from Jesus. The result of a focus on religion is that many give up on God, equating a judgmental religious church with how God feels. Religious churches are not appealing because they do not represent the true heart of Jesus. Religious churches are full of what Mike calls "the leaven of the pharisees." Religious churches rarely tell the truth that religious activity cannot today or ever please God.

I Hate Religion challenges us to recapture a more Christ-centered attitude towards church by exchanging "religion" for "relationship," exchanging "performance" for "unconditional love." The result is a relationship with Jesus that allows us to know Jesus and love Jesus for who He is.

If you are a person who has been burned by a church or you are a person in the church struggling with what the church should and should not be, *I Hate Religion* is for you.

Rev. James E. Swalm Jr., Ph.D.
Senior Pastor: Red Lion Evangelical Free Church

INTRODUCTION

James 1:27 says, "Religion that is pure and undefiled before God, the Father, is this: to visit orphans and widows in their affliction, and to keep oneself unstained from the world."

Sadly, this is not what we think of when we hear the term *religion*. For many, religion is the very reason they quit attending church and gave up on their faith.

Welcome to *I Hate Religion*. To those of you who picked this book up and have been burned by a religious church that made you feel bad because of what you wore or because you had a different style than them, I apologize for that experience and I want you to know that Jesus is nothing like the judgmental experience you had.

CONTENTS

CHAPTER I

The Rules of Religion

The summer after high school, I started talking a lot with the youth director at my church. We would hang out at Applebee's and have late night talks, and he listened to me. He let me ask questions, debate things ... basically be real about the questions I had in regards to my faith.

Between discussions with him and my Dad, I got closer and closer to God. My family and I also started to think about what I wanted to do as far as a career goes. I had previously been thinking about business and during that summer I attempted to start my own painting business and a business selling sunglasses, all in order to work my way through school.

I decided within a matter of days that I was going to just head down to Florida and take a year of Bible courses. Spending time with God on the beach sounded like an okay plan. So three days later my Dad and I packed up my Cadillac and drove to Florida.

However, I wasn't prepared for how strict this one-year Bible college would be.

RULES UPON RULES

My main reason for attending this school was that it was near the beach. That was the extent of it. I quickly found that they had rules for everything, and rules about physical contact between boys and girls was one of them. Well, I got in big trouble because I had a girlfriend and we met up to do laundry in the laundry room and got caught kissing.

Later that evening the dean rolled over in his golf cart, picked me up, and said he needed to talk to me. As we rode around campus in his golf cart, I was just waiting for him to lay into me. After several minutes of silence, he said, "So, how was it?"

I replied, "It was awesome."

Then he said, "Don't do it again."

I responded, "Okay."

He let me off the golf cart. He was pretty cool about things, but I can't say the same about everyone else there on campus.

> Is it possible we've followed all the rules and don't know God?

The school was extremely concerned with doing everything right, hence the mountainous rules and guidelines. One of the rules was that we had to spend time with God each day in devotions (reading the Bible and praying according to their prescribed plan). We actually had a "Resident Assistant" (RA) who would check our devotions to make sure that we were doing them and this RA would determine whether the devotions were adequate.

There was a day when I didn't do my devotions and the RA checked them. The RA said, "You missed your devotions."

I replied, "Yeah, I missed a day."

He returned, "Well, I guess you'll have to do two of them today."

I couldn't argue with the RA, but I thought to myself, "Two devotions! Seriously?"

This RA didn't get it. It wasn't, and isn't, about how many devotions you do. It's about spending quality time with God. That would be the equivalent of me missing a meal with my wife and saying, "Honey, I'm sorry I missed dinner last night, so tonight we are going to have two dinners. We'll go to Outback first and then we'll hit the Olive Garden."

How ridiculous! My wife doesn't want me to have two dinners, she wants me. She wants time with me. She wants deepness of a relationship.

God doesn't desire our rituals, our memorized prayers, our perfect attendance, our confessions, or our deeds. He desires our love. He wants us to love Him and He wants quality time with us. He simply desires us. So often we miss it because we get stuck in this trap of ritualism.

BASIC STANDARDS ARE GOOD FOR US

We have these basic standards that are lined out in Scripture. The basic standards are good for us. They are for our good. But what happens when we break a basic standard to do something even better? Well, the Pharisee (the religious person) can't possibly perceive of how this would be good because to him goodness and righteousness is found in adherence to those rules.

A group of us from school went to the beach one day. We were just hanging out, talking to a group of guys while playing guitar and throwing football on the beach and through the conversation we got on the topic of God and several of the guys came to faith in Jesus. It was an amazing experience that I'll never forget!

But when I got back to my dorm room, the RA asked me where I had been. I explained that I had been at the beach. "You won't believe this, but we talked to some guys and several of them came to faith in Jesus. It was an amazing night!"

The RA looked at me and said, "That's great Mike, but you do realize you are five minutes late for curfew, don't you?"

I was blown away. How could being five minutes late for curfew even matter when several people were introduced to their creator? Who cares about being five minutes late for curfew?

Would it have been better to have left the guys who were interested in talking about God so that I could make curfew? While answering questions about salvation should I have cut them off and said, "Sorry guys, the people back at school care more about me making curfew than about you knowing Jesus?"

> **Religion says the "good Christians" are the ones who follow all the rules.**

Religion says that at all costs you must stick with the rules. You can't break the rules. Following the rules is what it means to be a "good Christian."

PREOCCUPATION WITH ACCOUNTABILITY

Religious people are preoccupied with accountability. They don't miss the sin in another person's life. They are preoccupied with finding and "holding accountable" another person in regards to that person's sin.

Religious people feel good, spiritual, and acceptable when they can point out another person's sin. They see themselves as without sin in the same area.

This is why the religious person in your church is ready to pounce on the boyfriend and girlfriend who are sleeping together. They are thinking:

- They have to be held accountable.
- We need to do what's right.
- We can't just ignore obvious sin in the church.
- We can't compromise God's standards.
- God's standards are serious.

And the religious person ... is miserable, unfriendly, constantly gossiping, and on watch for the "bad people."

So what happens is that the religious person sees "bad people" as anyone who commits "bad sins" (sins that the religious person doesn't commit). The religious person creates a hierarchy of sins where everyone else's sins are really bad and need to be dealt with, while the religious person's sins aren't even sins at all.

RELIGIOUS PEOPLE LIKE TO PICK OUT A FEW SINS THAT THEY DON'T COMMIT AND RIDE THESE SINS WHILE IGNORING THE SINS THEY STRUGGLE WITH THEMSELVES.

What do religious people call their own sins? They call them "prayer requests."

But religious people fail to take an honest look at their own pride, arrogant judgments, and hurtful slander.

The couple that is living together are new to the church and are new to their faith. They are pumped about the church and they want to grow. But then they are slammed head on by the "mature" Christians who are ready to hang them out back behind the sanctuary.

Somehow it's easy to call out the "sleeping together issue," but you could never call out the religious person who has been in church for 40 years, trashes other people, and looks like they don't really know what salvation means because you've never seen them smile.

What's up with that? I'm not saying that premarital sex is Biblically okay, I'm just saying that religious people like to pick out a few sins that they don't commit and ride these sins while ignoring the sins they struggle with themselves.

BEING JUDGMENTAL

I invited a guy to church several years ago. He was a recovering cocaine addict who started to learn about God's love for him. He learned that God would accept him and forgive him in spite of his past failures, sins, and inadequacies. He was blown away that God would forgive him.

He couldn't get enough. Whatever I shared with him, he devoured it. After a Sunday message, he went up to the pastor and said, "Hey, that message or sermon or whatever you call it was pretty cool, man. For a pastor, you're cool as hell, dude!"

The pastor just smiled at him and didn't really know how to react. I was pumped that this guy came to church and that he was excited to learn more about Jesus.

Out in the parking lot, as he was getting into his car, a church leader walked up and banged on his window. My friend rolled down his window and the leader stated, "How dare you park your car in front of the house of God with a bumper sticker like that!" (The bumper sticker had "bad words" on it).

Politely, my friend asked, "Well, where should I park it, sir?"

He was promptly told, "Park it in the middle of the street for all I care!"

How's that for "come again next Sunday"?

Religious people are so ready to deal with all the sins around them. They are instantly ready to call out all the sinners. They don't feel it's right for people to get away with things. They burn "bad" music CDs and tell others that they can't play cards, go to movies, or play basketball on Sunday. And if you do any of these things, your salvation — or at least your sanctification — is in serious jeopardy.

The religious person might be thinking, "I don't do any of these things. I spend hours debating infant baptism and free will vs. predestination. I'm the good person who prays for all the sinners."

Yet his wife and kids are afraid of him because he has an anger issue.

Sound familiar?

From my frequent interactions with the recovering religious, this is all too familiar.

CHAPTER 2

The Religious Hypocrites

Be careful of religious hypocrites. I'm warning you.

When I first started tackling this issue of religion and talking about how people had been burned and hurt by religious people, I could tell that it made other pastors uncomfortable. But the more I simply shared Jesus' perspective, the more these same pastors rallied around the truth.

BUTTING HEADS

Jesus was constantly butting heads with the religious leaders of the day. The leaders focused on the rules and rituals, but Jesus was concerned with people's hearts and relationships.

What's amazing is that in Luke 12:1-3, Jesus has thousands of people gathered together. The Bible says they were trampling each other. They were literally stepping on each other to get to Jesus. They wanted to hear Him, to hear what He had to say.

And Jesus, with thousands of people gathered around Him, looked at the disciples and boldly said, "Beware of the leaven of the Pharisees, which is hypocrisy."

What did that mean? Jesus was warning the disciples to watch out for the religious hypocrites. He was not afraid to approach this issue, even with thousands of people gathered around, trampling each other like they are at a football game.

Jesus just calls it out:

- Be careful about the religious hypocrites!
- They like to have secret meetings and gossip about other people.
- They love to watch for you to screw up and then nail you to the wall.

Sound familiar in today's churches? Without question.

But Jesus warned that they—the hypocrites—were sinning (hence the hypocrite comment) and that their sin was going to come out eventually.

CHRISTIANS PRETENDING TO BE PERFECT

I often hear people say that the community is turned off to the church because Christians are a bunch of hypocrites. We have all heard the statement, "The church is full of hypocrites."

But I really don't believe that the community that doesn't go to church has much of a problem with the fact that people in the church are hypocrites.

However, I do believe that the community gets angry at the Christians who are hypocrites and yet try to pretend they aren't. What's more, these same Christian hypocrites try to pretend they are perfect.

That is what I believe disgusts and turns off the community to the church.

The truth is, we are not perfect. We are all striving to grow and improve and learn, but we all fall short. We are incapable of fully living up to what we teach and what we know we should be doing. That is the nature of man.

> HYPOCRITES ARE NOT A TURN OFF TO THE LOST. IT'S THE HYPOCRITES WHO THINK THEY ARE PERFECT WHO ARE THE TURN OFFS.

Again, that isn't the issue. What angers the community and what turns people off to the church is not that you teach something and sometimes don't live up to it. Rather, it's that you don't live up to it and then pretend you are perfect.

Some not only pretend they are perfect, but they take it upon themselves to find all the faults in others, to call out their sins, and to make sure that the appropriate actions are taken.

Consider these words from Matthew 23:4-9; 13-15; 25-28:

> "They tie up heavy burdens, hard to bear, and lay them on people's shoulders, but they themselves are not willing to move them with their finger. They do all their deeds to be seen by others, For they make their phylacteries broad and their fringes long, and they love the place of honor at feasts and the best seats in the synagogues and greetings in the marketplaces and being called rabbi by others. But you are not to be called rabbi, for you have one teacher, and you are all brothers. And call no man your father on earth, for you have one Father, who is in heaven." (4-9)
>
> "But woe to you, scribes and Pharisees, hypocrites! For you shut the kingdom of heaven in people's faces. For you neither enter yourselves nor allow those who

would enter to go in. Woe to you, scribes and Pharisees, hypocrites! For you travel across sea and land to make one single proselyte, and when he becomes a proselyte, you make him twice as much a child of hell as yourselves." (13-15)

"Woe to you, scribes and Pharisees, hypocrites! For you clean the outside of the cup and the plate, but inside they are full of greed and self-indulgence. You blind Pharisee! First clean the inside of the cup and plate, that the outside also may be clean. "Woe to you, scribes and Pharisees, hypocrites! For you are like whitewashed tombs, which outwardly appear beautiful, but within are full of dead people's bones and all uncleanness. So you also outwardly appear righteous to others, but within are full of hypocrisy and lawlessness." (25-28)

Jesus was saying,

> You guys look so good on the outside. You clean the outside of the cup and it's sparkling and its clean and it's great looking ... but inside it's filled with maggots and worms and you make me sick.

> You may have fooled everyone else, but I know what's going on in your heart and it's not attractive at all.

WE ARE TO LOVE

Love is supposed to be the most sacrificial, giving, and dedicated thing. We are to love everyone around us ... but instead religious people love you to notice how religious they are. They love it when you see the "sacrifices" they have made, the dedication they have, and the price they've paid. They love it when you know that they are in fact the biggest financial contributors in the church, and if push comes to shove, they want you to know that if you vote against them or against their programs, then they may take their funds elsewhere.

Religious people want you to think that they go to every Bible study available every single week, that they are the ones who really love God, and that they aren't the ones who spend time with their families at home. After all, they reason, "The people at home with their families are obviously not as dedicated to God."

But this is what we (the "not so dedicated" people) see: religious hypocrites—who want others to think they are perfect—who drive cars with the Jesus fish or the "in case of rapture this car will be unmanned" bumper sticker and return home to their families they haven't seen in a week and somehow we are supposed to think that this is dedication, that this is spiritual, or that this is what God wants.

WHAT MOTIVATES YOU?
Our motivation should not be all about what others think. That means when we fast, pray, or give, we do not need to be seen by others. We are to do it out of our love and passion for God. Since we love God and genuinely love people, we pray for them, and we fast, and we give.

We don't need anyone to see it because the motivation has nothing to do with what other people think. Our motivation needs to be our love for Jesus and our expectation of great things. If you have to be seen by others for what you do, then your reason for doing it is not based on love for God. Rather, it's based on your desire for people to love you ... and that's calling it like it is.

Consider the following verses:

> "Bring no more vain offerings; incense is an abomination to me." — Isaiah 1:13

> "They have become a burden to me; I am weary of bearing them. When you spread out your hands, I will hide my eyes from you; even though you make many prayers, I will not listen" — Isaiah 1:14b-15

"Come now, let us reason together, says the Lord: though your sins are like scarlet, they shall be as white as snow; though they are red like crimson, they shall become like wool." — Isaiah 1:18

DO YOU DO THINGS OUT OF DUTY?

Do you view your relationship with God as a series of duties and tasks to be accomplished? It's an easy trap to get caught in.

For example, we often think we need to read the Bible in a year to be a good Christian, so we have our Bible reading plans and we read our allotment every single day ... not remembering what we read the day before. Then (God forbid!) we miss a few days and we try to cram three chapters in before the baseball game starts.

Or how about church attendance? We show up at church each week and therefore believe by being there every week that we are in good shape.

Or how about giving money? We donate a large amount of money and believe that we are making a big sacrifice and that we are now in good shape with God (kind of like those flowers you buy your wife when you have hurt her feelings).

WHAT is a relationship with GOD aLL aBOUT?

Or how about our clothes and our music? Maybe we wear certain clothing or listen to Christian music. If we do it, then we believe we are right with God.

As you noticed, the list was long ... but it could go on and on forever. You can easily come up with a huge list of do's and don'ts. Do this and this and this and this and this and don't do this and this and this and this. And the pile gets so large you can't see over it. You are overwhelmed, you feel like a total failure, and see no hope in being right with God. There's no way you can achieve it all.

Religion is exhausting, isn't it?

EARNING GOD'S FAVOR?

How is your joy? Do you have much of it? If you attempt to achieve through your own efforts a standard of performance in the hope that this will earn you favor in the sight of God and others ... think again.

Trying harder and harder and harder to make yourself better is never going to work.

Here is what seems to be bouncing around in our heads:

> "I'll come to church so I can be a better person."

> "God will be happy with me if I 'turn my life around' and start doing the 'right things.'"

> "God may forgive me if I beg long enough."

> "I won't feel like such a miserable failure if I pray just a few hours more."

> "Maybe God is angry with me ... I'd better work harder than ever before."

What happens? Exactly! We fail again and again and again. Despite the length of the list or the creativity of options, we will continue to fail to do everything just right.

Failure, especially as it relates to God, makes us feel incredibly insecure. We doubt whether we can really be saved. We doubt whether God really loves us. We know He is angry with us! And we really doubt that He accepts us.

We fear our own destiny because we know for certain that we have not performed adequately, much less the way we had planned.

Does that sound like you?

If so, then I'm guessing there is one more thing piled on top of the insecurities and questions. I bet you are frustrated. After all, you tried so hard, you had all the right intentions, and you feel like a total failure.

Congratulations, religion has just kicked your butt. It always wins, no matter how hard you try.

Sadly, people who start a relationship with God based on the sure-to-lose religious rules of ritualism will walk away feeling like a total failure. They will walk away, feeling as hopeless as when they came.

JESUS IS THE ANSWER

What you do for Jesus is never the answer. What you do to prove yourself is not the answer. Jesus is the answer. That's it!

Do you really think that beads or candles or church attendance or quiet time rituals or writing a big check or sporting a Jesus fish or some act of service is going to get you into heaven?

Honestly, answer that question.

How do I make God love me?

The truth is that Jesus dying on the cross for your sins and Him walking out of the grave is the only thing that you should put your trust in for heaven. The ONLY thing. Your performance will never be good enough, for it will (as you very well know) always fall short. If you could get to heaven by being good, why would Jesus have died on the cross? It makes no sense.

If you add works to grace, you lose grace. Anything other than Jesus and what He did for you will never help you, never. Religion gives people the false assurance that they are okay and right with God ... when they aren't.

CHAPTER 3

The Rarely Told Truth

The rarely told truth is that religious activity cannot, not today and not ever, please God.

Jesus addressed religious people who missed this point. We are all prone to do this … to keep trusting in our religion and our good deeds and our own efforts.

Matthew 19 tells the story that went like this:

> A man came up to Jesus asking what good deed he needs to do to have eternal life. So when Jesus spelled out the commandments there must have been a glimmer of hope in his eyes.
>
> The man said "I've done all these things, what am I missing?" And Jesus said, "Go and sell all you possess and give to the poor, and you will

have treasure in heaven; and come, follow me."
The man went away full of sorrow because he
had a lot of stuff.

Here was a guy who was religious. He had the rituals down and
he was a good person, but Jesus didn't want his religious exercise.
Jesus wanted a relationship with the man, to have him walk
beside Him, and for the man to give up the meaningless things
in life that he felt were more important than Jesus.

But the man didn't want to walk beside Jesus. Instead, he just
wanted to fulfill all his religious duties and to be told he would
be in heaven. Sadly, he missed it.

SALVATION BY EFFORTS?

Do you gain salvation by your efforts? Of course not. If salvation
has to be attained by my efforts, then I would go to hell. I can't
possibly be perfect, which is the standard.

Here's the deal: God's desire is NOT that I attempt to impress
Him with my good works. Not at all! He wants me to be
impressed by Him and to love Him and to desire Him and to
believe in Him and to follow Him.

The Bible says in Galatians 2 that:

> "A person is not justified by the works of the law but
> through faith in Jesus Christ, so we also have believed
> in Christ Jesus, in order to be justified by faith in
> Christ and not by the works of the law, because by
> works of the law no one will be justified."

You are not justified by your works either. Did you catch that?
Neither you nor I are justified or made right with God by works
of the law. So no matter how hard we try to perform all the works
of the law, no matter how many hours we dedicate to bettering
ourselves, no matter how much effort and energy and good
intentions we put into our time and our behavior, we cannot

make ourselves right with God. You can't do it and I can't do it. It's simply impossible.

Nobody who has ever lived and nobody yet to come will be right with God as a result of their stellar performance here on earth. You can't be justified by your works, so quit trying to be right with God by being good. You'll never do it. Your religion won't, and can't, save you.

JESUS DID ALL THAT WAS REQUIRED

I am convinced that religious ritualism is evil. The idea that you can make God love you by trying harder in church or by wearing the right things or by saying the right things or by reading enough or by praying enough ... it's pure evil! It's not the gospel at all.

The good news is that Jesus did it. He did it all. We don't have to make God love us because God loved us while we were sinners. He already loved us and will always love us. It's not even a question we should be worried about!

Jesus did all that was required to make us right with God. (One more time: He did ALL that was required!) He didn't do part of it so that we would have to finish the job. No, He did all of it.

Your job is now to love Him, know Him, draw near to Him, want Him, and desire Him. He doesn't want your good deeds, He wants you.

Despite what the Bible says, people naturally think, "Why can't I try harder?" Trying harder is what they are used to. It's what has become the normal operating procedure, but you need to know that whoever relies on the works of the law is under a curse.

Galatians 3 makes it very plain by saying that everyone who relies on the works of the law is cursed. You are cursed if you try to get to heaven by your religion. So if I try harder and attempt to do all the right things, then I am cursed. That's what the Bible says.

Maybe that's not what you learned in Sunday school when the teacher said, "Obey God and He will be pleased with you. If you listen to Him and do the right things, then God will be happy, and if you do the wrong things, God will be mad."

But the Bible says if you try really really hard to do all the right things you are flat-out cursed.

However Jesus doesn't end there because in His love He couldn't leave us cursed. We know we are cursed and we can't fix ourselves and religion can't fix us and we are a mess ... and then we learn that Jesus redeemed us from the curse of the law by becoming a curse for us when He died on the cross. Now THAT changes everything.

FORGIVEN AND FREE!
The curse is done for. Jesus ended it. You don't need to do anything. Jesus did everything.

Now, if you are like everyone else, you have probably thought, "Is it really done? Has my sin really been paid for? Am I really forgiven? I don't have to do anything?"

It is hard for us to accept that our sin is really dealt with and over and that we don't have to do anything else to be free.

Though we feel like we have to do something, God wants us to stop trying and to realize that Jesus already succeeded. Just look at Him in awe. Stare at the cross in amazement. Be blown away that He would rescue us from us.

WHAT THE LAW DOES
The law doesn't save us, but it does show us that we are sinners, and that is incredibly important. Sometimes I'll ask religious people, "How good do you have to be?"

The responses are all over the board. The problem, when it comes right down to it, is that law requires perfection ... and none of us are perfect. To say it again, the law doesn't save us, it just shows us that we are sinners.

Paul says that the law is a tutor or a teacher and what it teaches us is that we can't keep the law. We are sinners who are totally cursed. Romans 3:23 says that all have sinned and fall short of the glory of God. Therefore, any and every sin causes us to fall short of the glory of the sinless God.

> We don't have to work to make God love us, because God loved us while we were sinners!

What are the results of falling short? Quite simply, it means that because we are sinners we cannot have God. Jesus even explained that "unless your righteousness exceeds that of the scribes and Pharisees, you will never enter the kingdom of heaven."

If you still think that keeping the law will get you to heaven, think about the best person you know, the most religious person you know ... you have to be better than that great example. You have to be way better, you have to be perfect, or you will never enter the kingdom of heaven. And that is not possible, is it?

GOD ALWAYS DEALS WITH SIN

That is one thing about God, He always deals with sin. With all of your and my sin, and everyone else's sin in the whole world, He had to deal with it. He had to take care of it, or everyone would get what they deserve.

So He sent Jesus. This is why Paul said, "For our sake he made him to be sin who knew no sin, so that in him we might become the righteousness of God." We don't get right with God because of us, we get right with God because of Jesus.

Jesus is the only way to get right with God. In the Garden before Jesus was arrested, He cried out asking the Father if it were possible for people to be saved apart from the cross — essentially if there is any other way. But there was no other way. Jesus is the only way.

Jesus was perfect. Jesus was sinless. He asked to pay the penalty for our sins, to experience the wrath of God for all the sins we have ever committed, so that we could be forgiven, set free, and right with God! God is fair, and unlike our judicial system that doesn't always get it right, God always deals with sin. Because sin had to be dealt with, our sin had to be punished. When Jesus died, He paid for my sin so I wouldn't have to, so that I could be forgiven, and so that I could be rescued.

GOD WANTS US, NOT OUR EMPTY RELIGION
What's amazing is that Jesus broke the rules that the religious people had. He performed miracles and He did them on a day when nothing was supposed to be done. It was a day of rest.

The religious people were so stuck on the rules that they couldn't possibly see a scenario where anything other than following the rules could ever be good.

It's the same today. Religious people build their identity on their performance. They are:

- exhausted
- feel a ton of guilt
- worship God out of fear
- can't conceive of anything that isn't entirely rules
- believe everything is performance focused

This is incredible because I think we get it all wrong. We all tend to think this way, even if we aren't trying to. I was sitting in Starbucks one evening with a young man, just talking to him about how God really does love him and how Jesus died for him and how Jesus wants to know him individually. You could almost see, in cartoon-like fashion, the light bulb go off above his head. With great excitement, he said, "Wow, God loved me that much, and since He loved me that much and forgave me that much, I just want to do something to thank Him, to show Him that I love Him."

We don't do good things to make God love us. Because Jesus loves us even though we are bad, we want to do good things. Works are a response to grace. I don't do good things to make Him love me, it's because He loves me that much even though I'm bad … now I just want to thank Him. I am just blown away by His love and grace. It's a natural overflow out of our excitement for a God who loves us and shows grace to us.

THE CHRISTIAN VALUE PACK

It's not about what we DO, it's all about what Jesus DID. As Christians, we believe and we teach (correctly so) that we are saved by God's grace through what Jesus did on the cross. If we believe in Him and put our faith in Him, then we are forgiven and our sins are dealt with. We talk about grace, faith, and salvation being through Jesus alone and not as a result of our efforts.

And people put their faith in Jesus.

Then … almost the moment after they accept Jesus as Savior, we tell them, "Now, here's what you have to do." We give them a stack of stuff (the Christian "value pack") and tell them to go off and be a good Christian the rest of their life. Things like: read your Bible every day, pray every day, and then you are in good shape.

How GOOD DO YOU HAVE TO BE?

Suddenly grace goes right out the window. It was justification by grace, but we turn it into sanctification by works. It was all about what Jesus did, but we turn it into being about what we do.

From this launching pad, we are motivated to serve God in order for Him to be happy with us and to love us, all done so that we will be "good Christians."

But our motivation for serving Him should have nothing to do with making God love us. We should serve Him because He loved us first "while we were yet sinners."

YOU CAN'T IMPRESS GOD

Sometimes we get caught up in thinking that we are going to "impress God" or somehow do enough good that He will recognize it and grant us entrance into heaven. This is silly! It really is. Picture this: I help an old lady across the street.

Is God going to say to me, "Wow, Mike, that was impressive. You helped an old lady across the street. I'm going to stop focusing on making stars and rotating the earth for a second because what you just did is so amazing."

My point is that God does not want us to seek to impress Him. We can stop trying to impress Him. He simply wants us to be impressed by Him, to look at Him and be amazed. Jesus wants to be our treasure, our hope, and our joy.

THE ULTIMATE GOAL

What is the ultimate goal? It is to be crazy about Jesus. The ultimate goal is not to be more like Jesus. Have you heard that? I've heard it many times that our goal is to become more like Jesus. It sounds great, but I don't think that's our ultimate goal even though its great when it happens.

Our ultimate goal isn't to be more like Jesus. Our ultimate goal is to know Jesus, to love Jesus, and to come into a deep or deeper relationship with the God who made us and who loves us.

The goal is not improved behavior. It isn't to be a good person or to use God to be better. Our goal is to know Jesus, to fall in love with Jesus, and to be crazy about Jesus.

When you are crazy about Jesus, your life changes as a byproduct. When your heart is just to be close to Jesus and know Him and desire Him above everything else in this world, He will work in you. When you want to know His passion for you and you want to understand the cross on a deeper level, then change will happen.

Change or behavior modification is still not the ultimate goal. It's all about knowing Jesus ... but we are so quick to go back to the behavior thing. We go back to religion and law because it's ingrained in us.

ENJOY THE RELATIONSHIP GIFTS

A mother let her child play in the backyard while she cleaned the kitchen. After mopping and waxing the floor, in walks the child, tracking dirt across the floor, with a handful of flowers pulled directly from the mother's flowerbed. With a big smile, the child declares, "Mommy, these are for you!"

The mother took the flowers and treasured them. She was thankful for them because they were given out of love and the child was excited to give them.

> GOD DOESN'T WANT US TO TRY TO IMPRESS HIM, RATHER HE WANTS US TO BE IMPRESSED BY HIM.

Know that God is not looking to pounce on you because you walk in with dirty feet. He wants you to know Him and love Him. He wants your love, your relationship.

The common thing I hear in talking to teens is, "We don't care about mom or dad buying us things, we want to spend time with them" and "I want dad to be around to play catch" and "I want to do something with my mom."

This is why Jesus told the crowd and His disciples to come after Him, to deny themselves, to take up their crosses, and to follow Him. Notice He didn't beg them to attend the synagogue, to give more money, or to be nicer to their families.

31

He told them, in essence, "Come, follow me. Come be with me. Know me, love me, desire me, walk with me, live with me. I want a relationship with you. I want your heart and your devotion even if it means dying for me. I want you to love me with all that you are. I don't want your religion. I want a relationship with you!"

Those aren't exact words from the Bible, obviously, but it certainly conveys Jesus' heart!

GOOD PEOPLE VS. "BAD PEOPLE"

Jesus tells a parable about a religious person in Luke 18:9-14. Luke explains that Jesus told this story to people who trusted in themselves and who thought that they were good people and right with God, but who treated other people poorly.

In the parable, there is a man who comes into the temple to pray. He's a pharisee. The second guy who comes in to pray is a tax collector. So you have a religious guy and a guy who is not only non-religious, but people don't like him because of the job he has.

Jesus wants to be everything for us.

The pharisee literally thanks God that he isn't like the tax collector, one of the "bad people" in the world.

We often think there are two categories: "bad people" and "good people." It's this type of thinking that causes parents to think they should shelter their kids, keeping them away from the "bad kids." I've had parents ask me if a certain child is going on the trip. If so then their kids aren't going because the parents don't want their kids to be corrupted by the "bad kid." But the two categories are not "bad people" and "good people" they are "bad people" and "bad people" who have trusted in Jesus. We are no better... your "good kid" is probably worse — they just hide it well.

The religious guy, the pharisee, is glad that he isn't like the non-religious guy who does bad things. Not only is the pharisee not bad, he's really good. He's the guy who is really involved in the church and gives a lot of money!

The tax collector in the parable won't even lift his head. He just beats his chest and asks God to show mercy to a sinner like himself. He realizes and recognizes that he's a sinner. He knows he cannot do it on his own. He cannot start "being good" like the pharisee. He's utterly hopeless, totally ashamed of his sin, and he simply wants God to show him mercy.

Jesus explains that the tax collector, rather than the pharisee, went away right with God! That was huge!

What Jesus was saying is that the religious person walked away and was not right with God and therefore was not even really saved. The pharisee was trusting in his performance to make him right with God and he couldn't get past his own performance.

The tax collector, on the other hand, was ashamed of himself and poured his heart out to God. He knew he was a sinner and that it was all about God, not the tax collector's performance. It was actually the tax collector who was saved, not the religious "good guy."

GOING THROUGH THE MOTIONS

It's amazing that we can go through all the motions and miss it altogether. We attempt to do all the right things to make God happy.

Remember the story about Martha in the Bible who runs around doing all the stuff, going through the motions, and Jesus said it was better just to sit in front of Him, to spend time with Him, to worship and know and love Him, like Mary did. He wants to be everything for us.

Don't go through the religious motions anymore. The empty prayers and religious actions, they make God sick. He wants us, He wants you. He wants a relationship with you. It's time to go against the flow and follow Jesus!

CHAPTER 4

Religion Has Style Points

We get too caught up in things, like looking and sounding spiritual. I used to joke with my sister that people would walk through the doors of the church and start speaking another language.

"How art thou, Mike?"

"Bearing many burdens John, how about thee?"

And people would talk that way and it sounded really spiritual, but it was really hard to even know what anyone was saying.

WHAT DOES IT MEAN?
I even asked a Sunday school class one time, "What does 'amen' mean?" The whole class just looked at each other. Even the

teacher didn't know what it meant. I then asked, "Why do we say something if we don't know what it means?"

What if it means "just kidding" and after every prayer we were saying, "just kidding"? We wouldn't even know because we never took the time to find out what the word means.

I think God wants us to be genuine and not just say things because we have always said them or because the religious people around us say them.

So I told the group that I was going to say, "Talk to you later," at the end of my prayers. After all, I say "talk to you later" when I end conversations with my parents. It's genuine, and it's me, so why not say "talk to you later" after prayers.

Do you KNOW WHAT you are saying?

I began saying "talk to you later" after my prayers. The problem is that people would still keep their heads down because they thought I was still praying. So I would just say "amen" after "talk to you later" and their heads would come back up. I learned that "amen" means that the prayer was over and you could open up your eyes. I later discovered that "amen" meant "so be it" or "let it be so." And as a side note, saying "talk to you later" is not irreverent or ungodly, it's genuine communication to God from my heart.

PRAYING WELL?

I hear people say things like, "I don't pray as well as that person does." Pray as well? Prayer is a conversation with God! Its not a better or worse thing. It's you talking to God, being real and being genuine. How can one person do it better than another?

Most people feel like they have to pray like Greg does in the movie *Meet the Parents*. It's this type of churchy language style and attitude that makes people feel inferior about themselves and afraid to be passionate about God.

MONOTONE FOR JESUS?

I remember many years ago looking around and realizing that everyone looked really proper, but they also looked really bored. I was thinking to myself, "Jesus died on the cross and saved me from my sins. I am pumped! So why does everyone else look so dead?"

The pastor was standing there with a monotone voice saying, "Jesus rose from the dead." Jesus rose from the dead and you have a monotone voice about it? You don't see a football player marching into the end zone in the Superbowl and the announcer say in a monotone voice, "And he's in for the touchdown."

The tone should match the significance of the event. When you realize the truth of what you are talking about, it should come out. The church claims to connect with the God of the universe, so why does it feel like death in there?

Ezekiel 16: 10-15 says,

> "I clothed you also with embroidered cloth and shod you with fine leather. I wrapped you in fine linen and covered you with silk. And I adorned you with ornaments and put bracelets on your wrists and a chain on your neck And I put a ring on your nose and earrings in your ears and a beautiful crown on your head.

> "Thus you were adorned with gold and silver, and your clothing was of fine linen and silk and embroidered cloth. You ate fine flour and honey and oil. You grew exceedingly beautiful and advanced to royalty. And your renown went forth among the nations because of your beauty, for it was perfect through the splendor that I had bestowed on you, declares the Lord God.

> "But you trusted in your beauty and played the whore because of your renown and lavished your whorings on any passerby; your beauty became his."

Ezekiel 16:48-50 declares,

> "As I live, declares the Lord God, your sister Sodom
> and her daughters have not done as you and your
> daughters have done. Behold, this was the guilt of
> your sister Sodom; she and her daughters had pride,
> excess of food, and prosperous ease, but did not aid
> the poor and needy. They were haughty and did an
> abomination before me. So I removed them when I
> saw it."

They trusted in their image rather than truly having a love and passion for others. God removed them when He saw it. That's a big deal. We love to look really good and show up in church and feel really spiritual, but if we look really good and sound really good and dress really good and yet we don't aid the poor and needy or love the unlovely, then maybe God will remove us too … or maybe He should.

Christians have a reputation for judging others. I tend to think that Christians judge others in order to feel justified for not helping. They know they should be helping but they really don't want to.

Are churches guilty of looking really good, dressing really great, and not aiding the poor and needy? Yes, of course they are!

How do we justify this inaction? We make statements like "Well, if we give money to the poor guy, he's just gonna spend it on cigarettes or beer."

THE POOR GUY WILL JUST SPEND MY MONEY ON BEER OR CIGARETTES.

And then we feel better about passing by on the other side of the road like the two religious guys who preceded the Good Samaritan. It's a shame that we actually feel good about it. If the man with the stained t-shirt is not as loved and valued as the man with the nice suit and the highlighted Bible, then we aren't looking at people the way Jesus looked at them.

Who did God choose to lead the nation Israel out of Egypt? He chose Moses, a guy who likely had a speech impediment. He didn't pick the strong, handsome, articulate motivator. God loves to use the unlikely people to do great things. We love the style and the flash. We instantly assume that woman wearing a nice dress who is super smiley and has a huge Bible must be a big-time Christian.

ARE PEOPLE AFRAID OF US?

I was shocked when I heard that some people are afraid to come to church because they think they won't be accepted if they don't have a suit. It makes me sick that people feel that way. Seriously, people sit home and feel unworthy to come to church because they can't match the dress, the language, or don't know the Lord's prayer by heart. That's sad!

I was at the grocery store and the cashier asked me if I was the Pastor up at Cornerstone. I said I was and she said, "I heard you were a different kind of pastor."

Not sure if that was a good or bad thing, I said, "Well, you should come on out to church some time."

She replied, "Oh no, I'm not going to go to church. I went to a church in town and the pastor called me out during his message and said, 'How dare you wear jeans in the house of God.' I left and never went back."

I was shocked. I still can't believe a pastor actually said that!

So I told her, "If you come to church this Sunday, I will wear sweatpants."

She couldn't believe I would wear sweatpants, but that's what it took to break down that barrier. She came to church the next Sunday!

There are massive walls that have been put up that keep people from even considering Church or God or Christians. They are walls of religion, and Jesus doesn't like the walls.

1 Corinthians 1:26-29 plainly states,

> *"For consider your calling, brothers: not many of you were wise according to worldly standards, not many were powerful, not many were of noble birth. But God chose what is foolish in the world to shame the wise. God chose what is weak in the world to shame the strong; God chose what is low and despised in the world, even things that are not, to bring to nothing things that are, so that no human being might boast in the presence of God."*

DO WE GET "STYLE POINTS"?

The pharisees had "style points." They looked really good, wore the right clothes, talked the right way, and said the right prayers, but Jesus didn't choose the Pharisees to be His disciples. Jesus didn't pick the religious leaders of the world. He chose the regular guys, the stinky fishermen.

I can see the wisdom in this because the people who cause the most problems tend to be the ones who grew up in church. The new Christians are simply excited about Jesus, but it's the religious people who can drive you nuts.

It's true that religion might have style points, but Jesus doesn't care about style points. Jesus likes to use the most unlikely of people. He likes to choose the weak things in the world to shame the strong, which is why He loves to use the low and the despised.

IS WORSHIP A MATTER OF PREFERENCE?

In our churches today, it needs to be stated very clearly that one style of worship is not superior to another. The traditional style of worship is not superior. We can have different preferences, different styles, and different tastes, and having a specific style or taste is not right or wrong, it's just a matter of preference.

This means that it's not bad to get dressed up. You can wear whatever you want. It is bad, however, when people think that getting dressed up is getting them closer to God or making them superior to someone else. I don't mind that you wear a suit, just don't send me an email telling me that I have to wear a suit or that I don't love God as much as you because I don't wear a suit. And I promise that I won't send you an email telling you that your suit is evil. Deal?

It's also important for contemporary people to remember that contemporary style is not superior, and neither is casual dress.

CHRISTIAN T-SHIRTS & BUMPER STICKERS

Christian t-shirts and bumper stickers won't save you. I figure you know that ... but do you know that often it's the t-shirt and bumper sticker that turn off non-Christians? They read the words and they want to avoid you.

I saw a Christian t-shirt that said, "The bigger they are, the harder they fall," with a little David and Goliath picture. Or the t-shirt that reads, "Gone Fishing," with a subtitle, "for men." Or how about the one that was made to look like an Abercrombie and Fitch shirt and it says, "A-bread-crumb and fish." Or the "God answers knee mail" or "Global warming is nothing next to eternal burning" shirts.

I would like to rip off the shirts and tear them to shreds.

As for bumper stickers, have you seen the "This car is prayer conditioned" or the "God allows U-turns" or the "Suffering Truth Decay? Brush up on your Bible!" or the "In case of rapture this car will be unmanned" or the "God is my co-pilot" bumper stickers?

I want to rear end people with these bumper stickers.

YOU CAN'T CONTAIN GOD

No matter what you have heard or what you feel, God can't be contained by our personal style or preference. We can be trendy or traditional and still not have a heart focused on God.

Being trendy or traditional—without God—and all you have is a style with God added to it. But that's not God! He is not traditional and He is not contemporary. He can't be contained by your personal style or preference. God loves people of both styles.

God is never going to say, "Turn down those drums," but He is also not annoyed by traditional music either. Again, He is not a God of either styles.

Here's a novel idea ... "He is the God of all styles."

How is that possible? Well, God created us all unique with different tastes, likes, dislikes, and cultures. Revelation talks about people of all tribes, nations, tongues, and languages who will worship God. He likes variety. So let's not get into this trap of complaining about each other's styles. Instead, we should remember that we are here to worship God.

We do contemporary music at our church because we know that it will be most effective in reaching the most people for Christ in our area. It also happens to be a style that most churches are not using in our area. Our style is not superior—it just fits more people's taste in this area and more of the younger crowd that is not being reached now by most churches.

CAN YOU LAY IT DOWN?

Could you lay down your personal preferences for the sake of the gospel? That's a very big question.

If you go to Africa to reach Africans in the jungle, you don't use the pipe organ. Even traditional churches are usually fine with their missionaries using unconventional methods to reach the tribal people. Go ahead and paint your faces, wear grass skirts, and bang away on the bongo drums ... whatever it takes to connect with and reach the tribal people.

We have that mindset about global missions, but we don't think that way when we look out our front door. The reason we aren't willing to do that in our own neighborhoods is because we care more about our own taste than the mission of seeing people come to Christ.

Jeans or suit? You only cross the line if you wear nothing!

The spiritually mature people are not the ones who have to get their way all the time. They are the ones who are willing to lay down their personal preferences for the sake of the gospel, for the sake of the Great Commission.

We get so caught up in our style and our tastes that we think God only likes what we are familiar with. People go to a church when they are younger and they think that God is synonymous with their church experience.

For many, their church experience was not a good one. For many it was an experience of being looked down upon because of how they looked outwardly (i.e. jeans or long hair) or how their personal preferences (i.e. of liking the drums) were from Satan.

It's time to be real, to draw others to Jesus. We don't do it to get points ... we do it because we want to.

CHAPTER 5

Your Approach Is Not Superior

People get nasty about the style they want to see. They get nasty when they want things their way.

I was in a church where the pastor added a contemporary service. He decided to have the contemporary service later and move the traditional service to an earlier time. This would allow for families to have more time preparing the kids for church and many of the older traditional crowd got up earlier anyway.

We made the switch as a church and that Sunday I was standing in the back when one of the leaders of the church (an older elder) started trashing the senior pastor for changing the service times. What he said was very embarrassing and there were people around that could definitely hear what he was saying. Then the elder looked at me and said, "What do you think?"

I said, "You don't want to know what I think."

He replied, "No, tell me."

So I said, "You're a father, right? You're a husband, right? How would you feel if your wife and kids were standing in the back of the house trashing the type of father and husband you are? Well, how do you think God views you standing in the back of the church trashing the man that He has put into leadership here? I think that if you have a problem you should talk to the pastor. I'd be glad to go with you, but I think you should stop gossiping."

Choose to be humble.

You can imagine the man did not receive my feedback with a spirit of "teachability." He didn't like what I said, and after that, he didn't like me.

Romans 14:1-4 says,

> "As for the one who is weak in faith, welcome him, but not to quarrel over opinions. One person believes he may eat anything, while the weak person eats only vegetables. Let not the one who eats despise the one who abstains, and let not the one who abstains pass judgment on the one who eats, for God has welcomed him. Who are you to pass judgment on the servant of another? It is before his own master that he stands or falls. And he will be upheld, for the Lord is able to make him stand."

BE SLOW TO JUDGE

Religion attempts to take a hard stance on things the Bible does not take a hard stance on. There are Christians who believe it is a sin to drink alcohol or to get a tattoo. There are Christians who believe it is a sin to drink coffee inside the church or to wear jeans to church.

Romans 14 is clear that we shouldn't quarrel over opinions. It is clear in scripture that drunkenness is sin, but there is no clear passage against tattoos. Trust me on that. I used to think they were evil, but now I have one. There is no passage against blue jeans and there is no passage against coffee in your worship center.

We create lines of division where they shouldn't be.

We get caught up in our personal musical taste. I have heard people who just love hymns say that hymns are superior to contemporary music. The problem is that hymns use words that we no longer use in our common language, such as "bulwark" and "ebenezar."

I was in a traditional service and we were told to open up to a page in the hymnal. It was the song, "Sometimes alleluia." The lyrics said, "sometimes alleluia, sometimes praise the Lord, sometimes gently singing, our hearts in one accord." I thought to myself, "Sometimes? Sometimes alleluia? Sometimes praise the Lord? What happened to rejoice in the Lord always? We aren't supposed to praise the Lord sometimes. We are supposed to praise and rejoice in the Lord always."

But there are also contemporary songs that I'm not a big fan of lyrically. I think the line, "heaven meets earth like a sloppy wet kiss" doesn't really say much. What does that even mean?

My point is that the issue is not about musical style. The words are what is important, not the style. And even more important than the words is our hearts. We can have the style we are comfortable with and use the words we like, and yet our hearts can be full of evil, selfishness, and sin.

As I've said, we worship in our church with a contemporary style and approach. We noticed that many people, who don't come from a Christian background, were very self-conscious about singing out loud in front of people, much less raising their hands in worship.

We also noticed that people were easily distracted by those around them, specifically small children who were sitting or standing with their parents during the musical part of worship.

What could we do to help people focus on the words and less on their surroundings? In an effort to remove distractions during worship, we decided to turn the lights off during worship and just have side lights on (so people can find their seats).

This way we could keep the focus on the worship, remove distractions, and people wouldn't feel self-conscious about what others may be thinking about them. Plus, for a contemporary church, stylistically, people enjoy it.

Very soon after the change, a guy approached me and said, "Pastor, you need to turn the lights on during worship."

I said, "Why?"

He explained, "You need to turn the lights on during worship because we are children of the light and Satan is in the darkness."

I responded by asking him if we put more bulbs in the ceiling would we be more spiritual? Then I made the point that God's word is a lamp unto our feet and a light unto our path. I pointed out that God's word is symbolic of light to people who are walking in spiritual darkness. We are not more spiritual if we have more lights in our church. It's about our relationship with Jesus.

Of course he wasn't happy with that. Soon after he and several others decided to leave the church over the issue of lighting. These are the religious people. They look spiritually mature, they sound spiritually mature, but looks can be deceiving.

DIFFERENT APPROACHES TO PRAYER

When it comes to prayer, I have found that I am not a typical sit down and pray for an hour kind of guy. I enjoy sitting down for five minutes to reflect and pray, but I am what you might call an "ADD pray-er." I pray randomly throughout the day because if I were to sit down for several hours and try to pray, or pray before I go to bed, I would fall asleep or be distracted.

I used to think that I was sinning or that I was less of a Christian because I could not pray for hours at a time. Then I began to cling to the concept of praying without ceasing, to believe that it was okay that throughout the day as I see things that needed prayer, I could pray for them when they come to mind and continually thank God as I went for all the blessings He provides.

> I can't pray for hours straight. Instead, I pray all day long. And you?

Others like to sit down and pray for hours. I knew of a pastor who prayed for three hours a day. Praying in one sitting is not superior to praying throughout the day as you think of things. And praying throughout the day constantly over different things is not superior to sitting down and praying for hours. They are different approaches and work for different people. What is important is that we are praying to God through Jesus, that we are connecting with God and loving Him. Making that time for Him is so important.

A DIFFERENT KIND OF GUY

John the Baptist was a different kind of guy. Matthew 3:1-10 states,

> In those days John the Baptist came, preaching in the wilderness of Judea and saying, "Repent, for the kingdom of heaven has come near." This is he who was spoken of through the prophet Isaiah: "A voice of one calling in the wilderness, 'Prepare the way for the Lord, make straight paths for him.'"
>
> Now John wore a garment of camel's hair and a leather belt around his waist, and his food was locusts and wild honey. Then Jerusalem and all Judea and all the region about the Jordan were going out to him, and they were baptized by him in the river Jordan, confessing their sins.

> *But when he saw many of the Pharisees and Sadducees coming to his baptism, he said to them, "You brood of vipers! Who warned you to flee from the wrath to come? Bear fruit in keeping with repentance. And do not presume to say to yourselves, 'We have Abraham as our father,' for I tell you, God is able from these stones to raise up children for Abraham. Even now the axe is laid to the root of the trees. Every tree therefore that does not bear good fruit is cut down and thrown into the fire."*

John the Baptist did not look like a Pharisee and he didn't look like a modern day pastor. John the Baptist was a hippie in his time. He was a desert dwelling, in-your-face kind of teacher. He didn't fit the religious mold. He wandered through the wilderness wearing camel's hair and eating locusts and wild honey. Locusts and wild honey is what poor people would have eaten.

He certainly was not carrying the appearance of "Sunday best." And if he's interviewing for a position at your church, you probably aren't hiring him! He doesn't have style points, that's for sure. Jesus likes to use the unusual among us.

HANGING OUT WITH THE "LOSERS"
Matthew 9:9-13 says,

> *As Jesus passed on from there, he saw a man called Matthew sitting at the tax booth, and he said to him, "Follow me." And he rose and followed him. And as Jesus reclined at the table in the house, behold, many tax collectors and sinners came and were reclining with Jesus and his disciples.*

> *And when the Pharisees saw this, they said to the disciples, "Why does your teacher eat with tax collectors and sinners?" But when he heard it, he said, "Those who are well have no need of a physician, but those who are sick. Go and learn what this means, 'I*

desire mercy and not sacrifice.' For I came not to call the righteous, but sinners."

Jesus reclined, relaxed, and ate with the "losers," the tax collectors and sinners. He loved them, cared for them, and reached out to them. This is equivalent to going down to the pub for dinner and eating with the pub rats and crooked lawyers. Many of us might be saying, like the Pharisees, "I don't know Jesus that well, but you can tell a lot about a person because of who they hang out with." Jesus didn't care.

We SHOULD NOT QUARREL OVER OPINIONS.

Jesus loved these people. He invested in and cared about those the religious people didn't want to talk to. The religious people just couldn't go down to the pub. If I go to the pub, the other religious people might think I'm a drunk or they might think that I am okay with sin and religious people might start rumors about me. After all, I do want to avoid the "appearance of evil."

For fear of what others think, we allow masses of people to remain hopeless while we focus our efforts on buying cushier pew padding to comfort the judgmental hypocrites we are afraid might gossip about us if we really mobilized to connect with the unreached people in our community!

For more insight into the difference in approach from Jesus and John the Baptist, check out Larry Osborne's book, *Contrarians Guide to Knowing God.*

LOVE BEING AROUND SICK PEOPLE
I'm sure there are Christians reading this book who resonate with many of the things I'm sharing ... but they are nervous that I might be excusing sin or compromising. Recognize that I'm not talking about excusing sin. Instead, I'm talking about loving sinners and showing them hope.

Jesus' statement about the sick needing a physician is incredible. We don't want to be around the "bad people" because we don't want to excuse sin. That's like a doctor saying he doesn't want to be around sick people because he doesn't want to appear to be supporting disease. That's absurd! We should LOVE being around sick people. Our job is to show sick people the cure.

We SHOULD LOVE BEING AROUND SICK PEOPLE.

We say we love Christ, that we are sinners, and that Jesus offers freedom and forgiveness from our sin so that we can experience spiritual cleansing ... then how can we let sick people get sicker and avoid them? They need Jesus just like we need Him. I suggest that those with the cure need to enter diseased buildings and offer it.

Ultimately, God is concerned that people's hearts and souls are reached. Preference issues too often get in the way of what is most important. It doesn't matter if someone has a different style of dress or if they like to drink a beer and you don't or if they like a certain type of music you don't like or if they like tattoos and piercings and you don't. What is important is that people are dying and in need of hope. If we are caught up in our comforts and preferences, then we are off base.

Jesus cares about your heart. I hate that many have been hurt by religion in the past, and if you felt like you never fit in because you didn't dress like someone else or because you didn't know how to sound and look religious or because you committed sins they didn't commit or because they looked down on you for your mistakes and failures, then please do this: throw it out the window. Forget it. I'm sorry that religious people hurt you, but that is not God's heart. He loves you just as you are ... but too much to leave you there.

DEALING WITH SACRED CURTAINS

I remember some people at a church I used to be at talking about how uninviting our church looked. The paint job, the carpet, and the pictures looked like a shrine to a church that used to exist. There were pictures of the church from the 1950s and curtains that were clearly 30 years old and petrified because of sitting in the sun.

I'm serious about the curtains. You literally had to break them out of position because they had baked solid in the hot sun. They were light on one side (facing the outside) and significantly darker on the other side.

We often made comments that when someone would walk into our church it was like a time warp. We had a service labeled "contemporary" in a church that communicated to visitors that we had not left the building for at least a decade and that we couldn't possibly relate to someone who watches *American Idol* on TV because we have no idea what has happened in culture for quite some time.

So we decided we were going to change the curtains. I knew that anything involving change would be an obstacle for this group of individuals, but the church had fallen into a 20 year coma and they needed to wake up.

We had our job cut out for us. Fortunately I did a little research to find out who had made the curtains. The woman who made the curtains was a sweet old lady who made excellent apple pie. I asked her about the curtain change and she was totally cool with it. She said, "Oh yeah, those curtains are old, we should have taken them down a long time ago." So I was free. I removed the curtains and put them in the attic of the church that very afternoon.

The next day one of the leaders of the church approached me and he was furious. He demanded to know who had the audacity to remove the sacred curtains. He didn't call them sacred, but they were. I told him that the curtains needed to be replaced because they were old and we were trying to be more inviting to church visitors.

He said something about how the visitors can go somewhere else if they don't like our curtains. Then I proceeded to tell him that the woman who made the curtains was in agreement that they needed to be taken down. He still didn't agree.

This was totally unacceptable. I got so irritated. The church is not meant to be a country club. The church is not supposed to just be a social gathering. It's a family of people diving into their faith, encouraging each other to live out what they learn, and loving Jesus more deeply.

CARPET COLOR IS NOT SPIRITUAL

Church business meetings have a reputation for stinking. I remember business meeting Sunday as the Sunday I dreaded as a kid. It was boring, it was long, and people got angry. There were often fights about the most ridiculous things. Individuals argued about whether or not to have a popcorn machine at the church carnival.

Then there was the business meeting where the church decided it was going to change the carpet. The carpet was old and beat up and coming apart, so there needed to be a carpet upgrade. It was announced that the carpet would be upgraded and that the color of the carpet would no longer be red, but green.

WHAT ARE YOU HOLDING AS SACRED?

Of course any change is a tragedy but some create a greater emotional response. One man stood up in the meeting. His face was red and he stammered, "By changing the color of the carpet from red to green, you are taking the blood of Jesus out of the church." The blood of Jesus out of the church? Because of green carpet? Come to our church because Jesus' blood is in our carpet! How absurd!

It's easy to make fun of the carpet color issue, but we are so stuck on doing things the way it's always been done. We make non-issues into spiritual issues. That's stupid. We need to focus on seeing people come to faith in Jesus and having their lives transformed and not on silly arguments.

How do you think people who don't go to church view Christians after witnessing these things? If you are reading this and you aren't from a Christian background, please don't assume all Christians agree or are okay with what some judgmental Christians and churches do.

WHAT ARE OTHERS THINKING?

Religious people wander far from the Biblical text and create standards that they are comfortable with. They get fearful of other Christians and their perceptions because religious people care more about being seen as "good Christians" and "spiritual" than they do about truly connecting with and loving Jesus.

We shouldn't need others to be impressed with our spirituality because it's not about that; it's about knowing and loving Jesus. But people go crazy with their concern about what others think. Sure, even if you can live in the same house with your girlfriend and not have sex, it sure gives the appearance of evil. It's not a good idea, but Christians get really nutty about it.

> Religious people care most about being seen as a "good Christian."

The really strict Bible school that I went to my freshman year of college was a perfect example of this. My sister was visiting from Philadelphia and wanted to come see me (I think partly because I was going to school in Florida and the beach sounded great). Well, we wanted to go to the beach for the day and the school had this rule that guys and girls couldn't ride alone (one guy and one girl) in a car together.

Of course I attempted to break this rule by riding in the car with my sister to the beach. I was informed that I could not ride alone in the car with my sister because it gave the appearance of evil.

The appearance of evil? I couldn't ride alone in the car with my sister because it gave off the appearance of evil? What evil was going to be done by riding in the car with my sister?

Relax! What does the Bible say? I know you want to control behavior, but teach the truth, don't teach a religious system that controls people so that you don't have to worry about them.

Why? Because even if you can control behavior, you can't control their hearts. It's impossible to create a system that produces heart change. Only the Holy Spirit can do that. Only a relationship with Jesus can do that, not religion.

CHAPTER 6

Religion Puts God in a Box

I love it when I'm around town and I run into people who go to my church. The kids' reactions are sometimes so awesome. One boy was surprised to see me at the grocery store and said to his mom, "What is Pastor Mike doing here?" She had to explain that Pastor Mike had to buy groceries just like everybody else. Another time, a boy thought I actually lived at the church because every time he came to the church, I was there.

Similarly, many people only think about God as being at their church. They don't think about God being in their daily lives and they don't see Him in their normal activities. The only time they think about God or hear about God is at the church they attend. As a result, they think that God is whoever their church shows them God is. So whatever religious routines they go through or went through, it had to represent God because that's the only time they ever experienced God.

I remember being at a church when I was younger. The pastor was boring, I thought the music stunk, I was bored, and I wanted to go home. Actually, I wanted to go to my grandpa's house and play video games.

Then the pastor said something I'll never forget. He said in all seriousness, "Isn't this great? This is what heaven is going to be like. We will be singing these hymns forever and ever and it will never ever stop."

I was terrified! This sounded like a horrible experience. So this is what heaven is like?

But that same thing happens when we go to a certain church and believe that what we experience there fully represents God. Maybe we didn't like what we experienced there, so we just weren't interested in God.

But God is NOT your experience at whatever church you went to when you were younger. He is not confined to my church. He is big and great and you could never imagine how amazing and awesome He is.

We often put God in a box because it is comfortable for us. We think He fits nice and neat in our little religious boxes ... but He doesn't fit.

PUTTING GOD IN A BOX
John 4:7-25 tells a very interesting story:

> A woman from Samaria came to draw water. Jesus said to her, "Give me a drink." (For his disciples had gone away into the city to buy food.) The Samaritan woman said to him, "How is it that you, a Jew, ask for a drink from me, a woman of Samaria?" (For Jews have no dealings with Samaritans.) Jesus answered her, "If you knew the gift of God, and who it is that is saying to you, 'Give me a drink,' you would have asked him, and he would have given you

living water." The woman said to him, "Sir, you have nothing to draw water with, and the well is deep. Where do you get that living water? Are you greater than our father Jacob? He gave us the well and drank from it himself, as did his sons and his livestock."

Jesus said to her, "Everyone who drinks of this water will be thirsty again, but whoever drinks of the water that I will give him will never be thirsty again. The water that I will give him will become in him a spring of water welling up to eternal life."

We OFTEN PUT GOD IN a BOX BECAUSE IT'S COMFORTABLE FOR US.

The woman said to him, "Sir, give me this water, so that I will not be thirsty or have to come here to draw water." Jesus said to her, "Go, call your husband, and come here." The woman answered him, "I have no husband."

Jesus said to her, "You are right in saying, 'I have no husband'; for you have had five husbands, and the one you now have is not your husband. What you have said is true." The woman said to him, "Sir, I perceive that you are a prophet. Our fathers worshiped on this mountain, but you say that in Jerusalem is the place where people ought to worship."

Jesus said to her, "Woman, believe me, the hour is coming when neither on this mountain nor in Jerusalem will you worship the Father. You worship what you do not know; we worship what we know, for salvation is from the Jews. But the hour is coming, and is now here, when the true worshipers will worship the Father in spirit and truth, for the Father is seeking such people to worship him. God is spirit, and those who worship him must worship in spirit and truth." The woman said to him, "I know that Messiah is coming (he who is called Christ). When

> *he comes, he will tell us all things." Jesus said to her,*
> *"I who speak to you am he."*

Jesus broke the religious boundaries and talked to sinners, which to me makes a clear statement: It's not about where you experience God, its that you experience Him through Jesus! You don't have to experience Him a certain way, but you do need to know a certain person and trust in Him alone!

We believe that other people (i.e. the tie-wearing guy who has it all together and is walking into the building in front of us) can be close to God, but we think, "Can I be close to God? I'm just a regular person."

If you think there is a certain way to worship God and experience Him, then you need to know that heaven is full of variety.

VARIETY IS A GOOD THING
I don't think that heaven is going to be one big choir singing from hymnals ... nor do I think it's going to be a jam fest of people rocking out to new contemporary songs. Ask people from an African village church and they will tell you that they expect to see all of heaven worshipping God with the bongo drums, singing with passion.

We tend to think that the way we experience God—the spiritual experience we most connect with—is going to be what heaven is like. But in all reality, heaven is going to be full of variety from every nation, tribe, tongue, and language. And we are all going to be celebrating God with different styles, tastes, and preferences from different cultures and backgrounds. And what's amazing is that we'll never complain either.

We will have perfect minds that understand everything perfectly. There will be no religion and we will all have perfect relationships with God and with each other. There will be no more ritualism. Instead, it will be real, authentic passionate love for God and for other people.

GOD IS NOT ONLY IN CHURCH

Many people believe that God is only at church, as if He lives there, and that experiencing Him is limited to church activities. They feel that in order to connect with God they need to go to church small groups or attend a Bible Study or help with a ministry.

But what we often fail to understand is that God is around us at all times, always with us, and He never leaves us or forsakes us. What this means is that we can talk to Him anytime. We can connect with God in the car on the way to work in just as real of a way as we do on a Sunday Morning. We can experience God in the cubicle at work. We can connect with the King of the universe while mowing the lawn. We can connect with God while drinking coffee, sitting in a pub, taking our child for a walk in a stroller, or as we are stuck in traffic during the commute home.

This is a critical error that must be corrected. God does not just want your Sundays and He does not want your rituals ... He wants you.

Acts 7:48-50 says it this way:

> *"Yet the Most High does not dwell in houses made by hands, as the prophet says, "Heaven is my throne and earth is my footstool. What kind of house will you build for me, says the Lord, or what is the place of my rest? Did not my hand make all these things?"*

We get really weird about the church building. A traditional church I used to be a part of had some really fancy-looking couches in the lobby. I was afraid to sit in them.

No wonder non-religious people have trouble connecting at church. You go into a building and you are afraid to touch the furniture and people are using weird churchy language, wearing dressy clothes, or sporting t-shirts with tacky Christian sayings on them. Then you're told to meet in the narthex after church. The narthex? What's a narthex? Where am I?

IS GOD ATTACHED TO BUILDINGS?

It is important to understand that the church is not a building. The church is a gathering of Christians together. Religious people get really attached to buildings, believing that when you step inside of the building that you are in God's facility. That's why you can't bang up the walls or break things, or play dodge-ball, drink coffee, or eat trailmix.

But God doesn't live in that building any more than I do. Maybe the reason you connect God to that building is because that's the only place you see Him. Like the kid who only saw me at the church and was shocked to see me at the grocery store. I think many people only connect with God at church.

In truth, the earth is His footstool and the building itself is just a building. A building doesn't save, only Jesus saves. God is not contained in your building and you are not damaging His house by getting coffee stains on the floor.

What's more, God is not confined to your building. He's not in a box. He's way outside of the box. God said that earth is His footstool. God rests His feet on planet earth. Don't get too attached to your sacred building as if you might accidentally sit in God's seat or spill on His carpet.

CHALLENGING RELIGION

Do you remember Stephen from the Bible? He was killed for challenging religion. He told the people to stop trusting in their religion and to accept the savior ... but in their religion they rejected the Savior and they killed Stephen for it.

Years ago, I was on staff as a full-time Youth Pastor. The youth ministry was growing and exploding and I had all kinds of ideas, but my ideas were almost always shot down. I was left feeling like I couldn't do anything, I couldn't attempt anything, and I couldn't try anything. I was not a part of the elder board (the leadership board of the church).

One day the Senior Pastor told me that since I was always at the church and I had lots of ideas and that I was a pastor (the Youth Pastor) that it made sense that I become part of the elder board. He said, "Biblically, a Pastor is an elder, and I think you're doing a great job. I think it would be really good that you were a part of the board to shape the future direction of the church." I was in.

Jesus is always breaking religious boundaries.

Then he told me to go to the Chairman of the Elders and to tell him that the Senior Pastor sent me and to talk to him about being a part of the elder board. So I went to the chairman and told him that the Senior Pastor sent me. I explained that I felt like I had a lot to offer in terms of ideas for the future of the church and that I would consider it a great privilege to work with the team and help lead the church. I said, "Biblically, a Pastor is an elder, and I would love as Youth Pastor to serve in that capacity."

The chairman said, "Let me get back to you."

About two weeks later, I got a call from the Chairman of the Elders. He said, "Mike, you are right that Biblically a Pastor is an elder, so we decided to change your title from Youth Pastor to Youth Director."

I asked, "Are you kidding me?"

They weren't kidding! They were willing to change my title just to keep me off of the board. They didn't want change and they didn't want anything to be done that wasn't traditionally done. They didn't want to rock the boat. They wanted to make sure the traditions and approaches they were taking as a church would be preserved and no one with an opposing viewpoint would threaten that.

It was at that point I knew I was done there. It was only a matter of time before I would find somewhere else to go.

FRESH IS A THREAT TO THE OLD
A fresh approach to truth threatens long-established religion. It always has and it always will.

I think many people limit their view of God. They don't want to think about God outside of their own comfort zone. They love doing things their way, running church their way, preserving their religion, and more ... but anyone with a different perspective about God is not welcomed.

MANY PEOPLE BELIEVE THAT GOD IS ONLY AT CHURCH.

Those who want to limit change are very comfortable believing what they believe. They are comfortable ... even though they are lifeless. They have made the religious box so comfortable, padded, and decorated that they don't want anything to change what they have created.

Then along you come with your fresh approaches or angles to truth. That's a full-blown threat to their long-established religion. They are quick to tell you, "Well, this is what we believe" or "We'll get back to you" ... and they never do.

They aren't willing to consider that maybe what they have believed for so many years might not be 100% accurate. They would rather go on pretending there is no issue than think differently, create change, or leave the confines of the religious box they have built.

DOES YOUR THINKING LIMIT GOD?
We all have to be careful that we don't put God in a box when it comes to our thinking. Isaiah 40:21-31 states:

> "Do you not know? Do you not hear? Has it not been told you from the beginning? Have you not understood from the foundations of the earth? It is he who sits above the circle of the earth, and its inhabitants are like grasshoppers; who stretches out the heavens

like a curtain, and spreads them like a tent to dwell in; who brings princes to nothing, and makes the rulers of the earth as emptiness.

Scarcely are they planted, scarcely sown, scarcely has their stem taken root in the earth, when he blows on them, and they wither, and the tempest carries them off like stubble. To whom then will you compare me, that I should be like him? says the Holy One. Lift up your eyes on high and see: who created these?

He who brings out their host by number, calling them all by name, by the greatness of his might, and because he is strong in power not one is missing. Why do you say, O Jacob, and speak, O Israel, "My way is hidden from the LORD, and my right is disregarded by my God"? Have you not known? Have you not heard? The LORD is the everlasting God, the Creator of the ends of the earth.

THROW *away* THE BOX *a*ND FOCUS ON HiM.

He does not faint or grow weary; his understanding is unsearchable. He gives power to the faint, and to him who has no might he increases strength. Even youths shall faint and be weary, and young men shall fall exhausted; but they who wait for the LORD shall renew their strength; they shall mount up with wings like eagles; they shall run and not be weary; they shall walk and not faint."

Religion limits our thinking of God to our religious experiences. Consequentially many people have an incorrect and/or extremely limited view of God.

Instead, let God be the center of everything you do. Throw away the box and focus on Him.

CHAPTER 7

Religion Limits Our Effectiveness

There are a lot of people who don't see God's bigness and power and they feel that Christianity is for wimps. They believe that only weak emotional guys need Christianity and that it's just a support group for wusses. The usual tough guy response is that God is a "crutch" for the weak.

Anyone who believes this does not understand the power of God.

I admit that the paintings of Jesus as a very wuss-like guy don't help, and neither do the ones where He is holding a lamb. Now, I understand that Jesus is the "good shepherd," but I don't think He had a pet lamb that He carried with Him everywhere for pictures.

When was the last time you saw a painting of Jesus dealing with the religious people or driving the money changers out of the church with whips? I'm sure He smiled and laughed, but He was tough. What's more, He would have had to have been in good physical condition to endure the beating He did before the crucifixion without dying before He got on the cross.

We simply don't understand the depths of the gospel, that this gigantic God who makes earth His footrest has such a love and passion for us that He would insert Himself into humanity to save us. It just sounds crazy, doesn't it, that God would insert Himself into His ant farm to save all of us ants? The big God who created us, designed us, knows us (knows us better than anybody), and loves us, would do that? Wow!

A THREAT TO THE RELIGIOUS

Being religious has a way of limiting our vision, and as a result, it limits our willingness to grow, to change, and to mature. John (11:1-6; 11-15; 17-27; 38-44; 45-50; 53) tells a great story:

> "Now a certain man was ill, Lazarus of Bethany, the village of Mary and her sister Martha. It was Mary who anointed the Lord with ointment and wiped his feet with her hair, whose brother Lazarus was ill. So the sisters went to him, saying, "Lord, he whom you love is ill."

> But when Jesus heard it he said, "This illness does not lead to death. It is for the glory of God, so that the Son of God may be glorified through it." Now Jesus loved Martha and her sister and Lazarus. So, when he heard that Lazarus was ill, he stayed two days longer in the place where he was."

> "After saying these thing, he said to them, "Our friend Lazarus has fallen asleep, but I go to awaken him." The disciples said to him, "Lord, if he has fallen asleep, he will recover."

> Now Jesus had spoken of his death, but they thought that he meant taking rest in sleep. Then Jesus told

them plainly, "Lazarus has died, and for your sake I am glad that I was not there, so that you may believe. But let us go to him."

"Now when Jesus came, he found that Lazarus had already been in the tomb four days. Bethany was near Jerusalem, about two miles off, and many of the Jews had come to Martha and Mary to console them concerning their brother. So when Martha heard that Jesus was coming, she went and met him, but Mary remained seated in the house.

Martha said to Jesus, "Lord, if you had been here, my brother would not have died. But even now I know that whatever you ask from God, God will give you." Jesus said to her, "Your brother will rise again."

Martha said to him, "I know that he will rise again in the resurrection on the last day." Jesus said to her, "I am the resurrection and the life. Whoever believes in me, though he die, yet shall he live, and everyone hwo lives and believes in me shall never die. Do you believe this?" She said to him, "Yes, Lord; I believe that you are the Christ, the Son of God, who is coming into the world."

"Then Jesus, deeply moved again, came to the tomb. It was a cave, and a stone lay against it. Jesus said, "Take away the stone." Martha, the sister of the dead man, said to him, "Lord, by this time there will be an odor, for he has been dead four days."

Jesus said to her, "Did I not tell you that if you believed you would see the glory of God?" So they took away the stone. And Jesus lifted up his eyes and said, "Father, I thank you that you have heard me. I knew that you always hear me, but I said this on account of the people standing around, that they may believe that you sent me."

When he had said these things, he cried out with a loud voice, "Lazarus, come out." The man who had died came out, his hands and feet bound with linen strips, and his face wrapped with a cloth. Jesus said to them, "Unbind him, and let him go."

"Many of the Jews therefore, who had come with Mary and had seen what he did, believed in him, but some of them went to the Pharisees and told them what Jesus had done.

So the chief priests and Pharisees gathered the council and said, "What are we to do? For this man performs many signs. If we let him go on like this, everyone will believe in him, and the Romans will come and take away both our place and our nation."

But one of them, Caiaphas, who was high priest that year, said to them, "You know nothing at all. Nor do you understand that it is better for you that one man should die for the people, not that the whole nation should perish."

So from that day on they made plans to put him to death.

Simply put, Jesus was a threat to the established religion!

The religious leaders could not let Jesus go on performing miracles and gaining a following. They had to preserve the religious institution. They believed that nobody would care about Judaism and that nobody would follow them (the religious leaders) if everyone was off following Jesus. They were saying:

> "We have to do whatever it takes to preserve the religious system, even if it means putting Jesus to death. All these followers are believing in Jesus, and He is raising people from the dead and His following is only getting more intense. We have to get rid of Him or we are all going to be out of jobs."

Obviously those aren't their exact words, but it's a close paraphrase. The religious institution simply could not let Jesus live.

CHURCHES DIE RATHER THAN CHANGE

Many churches today are dying because they are unwilling to change. It seems hard to believe, but it's true, and this is not even a truth or message issue—it's a style and method issue. Churches would rather die off than change.

Many churches claim that the growing churches are "compromising to culture" as a reason for the growth. The dying churches pride themselves in saying, "We won't compromise, we won't water down the truth, we won't tickle people's ears." But saying its okay to drink coffee in church or wear jeans on a Sunday morning is not tickling people's ears!

Often the message is the same, but the methods and approaches have changed to reach a fast-changing culture of people. Still, many are so convinced that God is limited to our methods or styles.

What those stuck-in-the-mud churches are essentially saying to the community (those who don't have a relationship with God) is this: "If you want to know Jesus, then you have to stylistically—in both music and clothing—conduct yourself as if you were living in the 1960s."

That's absurd! People who don't come from a Christian culture or background then think that God isn't relevant to them. He's a thing of the past that old people and their old music listen to. He doesn't connect with them or relate to them ... because the church has made Him appear out of touch.

SUNDAY SCHOOL?

This will be a total shocker to some, but the Bible never mentions Sunday school. The Bible does not say that God established the church and that they began meeting for Sunday school.

Now for a period of time, Sunday school was a really effective ministry, but if your Sunday school is no longer effective, if your Sunday school only has around 15 people in it and you're a church of 500, then maybe it's time to consider a different approach to helping people grow spiritually.

It may be more effective with this culture to meet in homes and at restaurants, to build a ministry around relationships where you are hanging out with people, talking, connecting the Bible to life, and encouraging people. You can share meals together and be in the community at the same time.

> **Do you read your Bible ... so you don't feel guilty for not reading it?**

Many people don't want to show up at a classroom two hours before church and watch you make graphs on a chalkboard and have them memorize the books of the Bible in order ... but they really do want to learn about Jesus. They really do want to grow spiritually and they really are excited about their faith. Know that there is nothing wrong with changing your approach.

GOD'S BLESSING IS NOT A FORMULA

For some reason, we think that God's blessing is a formula. We think that we are supposed to memorize certain prayers.

That's what we had to do as kids and somehow we think that if we don't memorize our prayers that somehow we love God less or that we are less spiritual or God will judge us. Or maybe we think that if we don't light enough candles that we won't make some sort of eternal difference on someone's soul. Even though the Bible never says certain prayers or lighting candles will be magical, it's what we've always done so we just keep on doing it.

Some feel that if they don't sit in a box and tell someone all the bad stuff they've done that they can't be forgiven (others believe they can do all those bad things again as long as they come back to the box and confess them all). Others feel that if they don't go to church each week that they won't have much of a chance to get into heaven.

I used to think that being a spiritual Christian who loved God meant that you had to read a lot of the Bible every day. So the really spiritual people, the ones who really loved God, were the ones who could memorize the most verses. They must definitely be going to heaven!

So I figured that in order to be a better Christian, the least I could do was read a chapter of the Bible a day, so I would read a chapter a day ... but then I would miss a day. Of course I had to make up for it, so the next day I would read two chapters, or three, and it became a ritual.

What was even worse was that on the days I would remember to read my verse I felt like God loved me, but the days I didn't read I felt bad and thought He didn't love me. I ended up reading just to remove the guilt. Of course, the next day I didn't remember anything I had read the day before, but it didn't matter because it was helping with the guilt.

IT'S NOT THE QUANTITY
It's not the quantity, but the quality that matters when it comes to reading your Bible. God does not want you to read the Bible to remove guilt or to appear spiritual. He wants you to spend quality time with Him, so if it's a chapter and you love it and you can retain it and it's totally inspiring you, then great. Read on, but if it's a couple of verses, that's fine, too.

God isn't concerned with the quantity as much as He is with the quality. It's a relationship and that means quality time. When I began to view my relationship with God as quality time to reflect and soak in what I was learning, I began to read smaller chunks of the Bible, but I soaked it in more.

I got more excited about God and my faith and it began to change my life. I was no longer "doing my time" with God everyday. I couldn't wait for that time of the day. It wasn't structured or legalistic. It was quality time, reading the words from God.

In Isaiah, God says,

> "Bring no more vain offerings, your new moons and appointed feasts my soul hates, When you spread out your hands I will hide my eyes from you, even though you make many prayers I will not listen."

It isn't about going through the motions because God is not interested in our vain offerings. He wants our hearts. Going through the motions is not attractive to God. Who would enjoy that in any sort of relationship?

We don't want the love of our lives to "go through the motions" with us. We want the love of our lives to desire us, to spend time with us, and to invest into us because that other person cares deeply about being with us and loving us and knowing us. It's all about a relationship.

ARE OUR METHODS AND APPROACHES REALLY ALL THAT IMPORTANT?

God designed us for relationship with Him. He is not interested in us going through the motions any more than you want your spouse or loved ones to go through the motions with you. I'm thinking, "If your heart isn't in it, if you don't love me, it you don't value me and desire me, then don't waste your time." Don't you think the same thing?

The ritual of it means nothing. In fact, doesn't the ritual of it just offend you? It hurts, doesn't it? Following the ritual shows that the person cares more about making himself/herself feel better than about knowing and valuing you.

WHY ARE WE SO MESSED UP?
People really are confused about God. Why is that?

The reason people are so confused is not because God is confusing. Rather, people are confused because religion clouds things up and confuses them. It's not God who is confusing us, we are confusing ourselves.

Religion is man's system to try to understand God, but we must remember that it's a system that we made up. And the more we trust in this system to save us, rather than trusting in God to save us, the more confused and lost we will become.

Amidst all the confusion, how do we "get right with God"? People who don't know God, how do they have a relationship with Him? How do they move past the rituals and know Jesus and have purpose now and forever?

Admittedly, we are all bad. We aren't good. We screw up constantly. Even the good we do often has bad motives and we get ourselves into a huge mess. We ruin our personal lives. We are lonely, hurting, miserable, and empty.

> I love it that God has to deal with sin and injustice.

Even if everything seems to be going well, if we don't know Jesus, we have no greater purpose and we have no future. We have all sinned, we don't reach the standard, and we are imperfect. Because of that, we are unable to be with God. We have no future in heaven. Our future is to be separated from the perfect awesome God who has to deal with sin and injustice.

I love that He has to deal with sin and injustice. I love it because I have been sinned against and I have experienced injustice. None of us want someone who has harmed us or our families to be let off the hook! However, we do want ourselves and our families off the hook.

That's where the good news (aka gospel) comes in. Jesus literally takes us off the hook and puts Himself on the hook. I am not on the hook because God hung His Son on the hook in my place. This is incredible.

INSTEAD OF ME
Jesus took the wrath so I don't have to. He took it instead of me. In the courtroom of God, I stood guilty. I deserved to be separated from God. I deserved to pay for my sins. But Jesus stepped in the way during my sentencing and asked to take my punishment. Jesus died my death for me. The sin was paid for. The sin was punished. The one who got the wrath was Jesus and not me.

Then Jesus came back from the dead (like He said He was going to) and if we believe in Him, if we turn from our sins, we will be forgiven and be right with God.

ONLY Jesus came back from the dead.

Ephesians talks about being saved (or rescued) from sin by God's grace and that it is a gift from God. It's not anything that I do or that I can do. I simply receive the gift.

But if I don't receive the gift, if I just go on doing whatever I want or if I reject the gift, then justice must be done. If I don't accept Jesus' dealing with my sin on the cross, then I have to deal with my sin in hell.

So it's either Jesus or its me who pays for my sin, but someone has to pay. Grace says it doesn't have to be me. Grace means that Jesus paid my price. On top of that, Jesus wanted to take our sin and die our death and set us free. He saw the outcome and our freedom from sin and it brought Him joy.

Back to boring, binding religion. It clouds up the truth. It makes us think that religion has something to do with us being free, with us getting off the hook, but religion had nothing to do with it. Religion had nothing to do with grace!

Instead, "our" forgiveness and freedom has everything to do with Jesus. The law couldn't save us, religion certainly couldn't save us, and our good deeds could do nothing to save us. Only Jesus could rescue us from ourselves and from the justice we deserve as a result of our sin.

Thank God for His love for us!

CHAPTER 8

Religion Ruins Relationships

Our ultimate goal as Christians isn't to become more like Jesus. Our ultimate goal is to KNOW Jesus. Religion's goal is that people would "become more like Jesus." Behind this is the strong desire to improve behavior. It's as if my ultimate goal is to "be good." This is so subtle and sounds so good, but it's at the core of a wrong focus for us as followers of Jesus.

Our ultimate goal is not to become more like Jesus in our behavior. If our ultimate goal is to become more like Jesus, then ultimate success would be perfect behavior.

Instead, our ultimate goal is not to behave more like Jesus. Our ultimate goal is to know Jesus. Religion wants us to focus on changed behavior, good actions. But God isn't interested in our less-than-perfect behavior, He wants us to love Him and know Him and desire Him and draw close to Him.

We do want to become more like Jesus when it comes to loving God, but our ultimate goal is not being better. Our ultimate goal is to know and love and value and desire and run after and have as our trophy and prize Jesus Christ. We can be religious and look more like Jesus in our actions and still not know Him. That's a sad reality for many people.

GOD WILL CHANGE YOU

A relationship with God will change you, He will change your behavior and everything about you.

Religious people can't help but focus on the wrong that happens in culture and the bad attitudes or sinful actions of people. They want to create a change, but in attempting to create change they target behavior. They focus on how they can change your actions. The problem is that behavior is only a symptom of a much larger issue.

ReLiGious peopLe TaRGeT BaD BeHavioR.

The larger issue is that people walking in sin are in need of a relationship with God. And because they don't have a relationship with God, they oftentimes don't want to behave the way the religious demand.

What should the religious do? The answer is obvious: Do not waste energy trying to change behavior. Instead, invest energy trying to connect the sinner with God—the God who loves us all despite our sins, failures, and inadequacies.

When sinners come in contact with God, lives will change. But again, behavior change isn't the ultimate goal. What's most important is that sinners are coming to know the Creator. It is through a relationship with the Creator that they will find purpose, joy, and a reason for living.

DO YOU LOVE JESUS?

I know a lot of religious people who don't love Jesus. They love good behavior and they love their rituals, but are they passionate about Jesus? Are they in love with Jesus? No. They just want you to shape up. They just want to make sure that they did everything on their spiritual checklist: attend church, say prayers, do good deeds, give money to poor people, and avoid all the bad people.

Religious people simply fail to recognize that they desperately need Jesus to set them free. They are messed up and in bondage, just in a different area than the sinner who walks in off the street.

When we try to change behavior instead of introducing someone to Jesus, they naturally resist us. They don't care about our morals and values. Frankly, they are turned off to us and to God in general whenever we target their behavior.

Instead, we should show them that their sin and the passionate pursuit of sin will not fulfill them ... but neither will good behavior. The only thing that will fulfill them or bring happiness is knowing Jesus.

We need to show them that the outcome of living out their sin-saturated lives is pain, misery, grief, and regret. The answer is to quit going after them and to go after Jesus. Change the object of pursuit. The answer is not to just quit pursuing things that aren't Jesus and to be good. The answer is to turn from those things and to pursue Jesus.

WHAT THE RELIGIOUS FEAR

Religion causes us to focus on being good and improving behavior and crossing off the two checklists we have, the "do list" and the "don't list." If we perform well, then we are good with God. It's important not to get sidetracked by the sinners, since bad company corrupts good morals.

So in order to not be corrupted, religious people isolate themselves from the "bad people." That explains how Christians can live in the community and yet the community doesn't even know them. In an effort not to "become like them," the Christian community becomes a sub-community within a community.

Christians live in fear of what others might think about them if they are seen hanging around with the "bad people," but their fear drives them to become ineffective in actually being a light in the community. They think that if they spend time with the "bad people" that they may be accused of being just like them ... and it's true. If we spend time with them then we probably will be lumped in with that group. Jesus was lumped in with that group.

I am not suggesting that you compromise living for God, but I am suggesting that you live for God in the midst of the world and that Christians don't isolate themselves from others.

One public school administrator said to a group of Pastors, "Stop taking the light out of the school." He was saying that public school kids need to be impacted by Christian kids. I understand there are numerous reasons for parents to send their kids to private Christian schools or to homeschool their children, but if we do it in order to hide from the "bad kids" or to separate ourselves from non-Christians, then we are taking the light out of the schools.

I think Satan would love it if all the Christians stayed away from the non-Christians. If the Christians stay away from the non-Christians, then they won't impact the non-Christians.

QUICK TO JUDGE
Religion causes Christians to ruin relationships with other Christians. Jesus said,

> "Why do you see the speck that is in your brother's eye, but you do not notice the log that is in your own eye? Or how can you say to your brother, 'Let me take the speck out of your eye,' when there is the log in your own eye? You hypocrite, first take the log out

*of your own eye, and then you will see clearly to take
the speck out of your brother's eye."*

We are so quick to judge others, but Jesus is reminding us that we, too, have sin in our lives. We are ready to point out the areas where other people fall short, but we haven't examined all the sin in our lives.

I remember hearing a pastor come down hard on the issues of drinking and smoking and bad music. He was just attacking anyone who would get drunk or smoke or curse. It was aggressive. He was fired up, his face was red, and his palms were sweaty. He wasn't going to "water it down." It was intense. It was pointed. And it was hypocritical.

The pastor who was speaking out against the drunkenness and the smoking and the cursing was making the case that our bodies are a temple of the Holy Spirit and that we should be taking care of our bodies. He repeated that over and over, but I had a hard time listening to him because he was extremely overweight (he had bad eating habits and didn't exercise).

> SATAN LOVES IT WHEN CHRISTIANS STAY AWAY FROM NON-CHRISTIANS.

So the pastor was talking about taking care of our bodies and yet he wasn't taking care of his own body. He specifically pointed out all the "bad sins" like drunkenness, smoking, and dirty words, but he never brought up the sin of overeating. He had a tree trunk growing out of his eye and he saw the sins of everyone else, but wouldn't admit his own.

At another event I remember a dynamic speaker who struggled with his weight and made the point that we all have sin that we struggle with. He said, "I can't hide mine, but many of you hide yours. It's important that we all deal with the areas of sin in our lives and encourage each other to turn to God for hope in those issues." I have a great deal of respect for that man. His message that day impacted me.

SUBTLE SINS

We must understand that none of us are innocent. It's so easy to come down on the sins that aren't the ones you struggle with, but when does anyone talk about the subtle sins, like pride, arrogance, unbelief, gossiping, and slander?

When was the last time you admitted to your spouse that you were wrong or had a bad attitude or said something in a harsh tone? When did you not attempt to make excuses but simply apologize and take full responsibility?

What about gossip? We hear, "Let's pray for Jen because I saw her meeting a guy at lunch who wasn't her husband," from a friend, only to find out later that Jen was discussing work with a co-worker or catching up with her cousin or meeting an old friend and her husband was okay with it.

But we already got on the phone and passed the word to everyone on the prayer chain (it's really just a gossip chain). It's divisive and it's wrong, but it happens all the time.

The sin of pride resulted in Satan (Lucifer) falling from heaven and Adam and Eve, who wanted to be like God and disobeyed, being cast out of the garden. Pride is a big deal! But most of us would not even think about correcting a prideful person or a gossip. We don't come down hard on the sins we commit. In truth, we need to be consistent, since we will be judged with the same measure of judgment in which we judge others.

YOUR OWN EFFORTS

We are all sinners, but religion tries to create a system that makes you think the solution to your sin problem is found in your efforts. But it's not your efforts that will help you, only the forgiveness of Jesus will help you.

Forgiveness is a huge deal. When Peter asked Jesus how long he had to forgive his brother and if seven times was sufficient, Peter was looking for an out. He was thinking, "I'll forgive him so many times and then I'm gonna stop talking to him, I'm going to stop forgiving and loving him." Jesus responded by saying, "I don't say to you seven times, but seventy times seven."

Churches should be known for their forgiveness, love, and grace ... but that isn't the case.

Are we supposed to forgive someone 490 times (70x7) and then we don't have to forgive them any more? If your wife has wronged you 480 times, does that mean she has 10 more left and then you don't have to forgive her any more? No! The idea is that we never stop forgiving. We don't keep tabs of the seven times someone sins, we just keep forgiving them and forgiving them and loving them in spite of their sins. This is exactly what Jesus did for us.

It's very comforting that Jesus loves and forgives us and there is not a number we can't cross. He just keeps forgiving us.

YOU SHOULD BE KNOWN FOR YOUR FORGIVENESS, LOVE, AND GRACE.

That's not religion, that's love, compassion, and grace. The church should be marked by Christians who are forgiving and loving each other, not looking to get each other. People are not perfect. That's why we need a Savior.

The people in church are not perfect either. When you go into a church, you are not going to be surrounded by perfect people who won't disappoint you. You will see many of the same broken people you see at work (or people like them), only they are in church with you looking to the perfect Savior for help and guidance.

Be ready to forgive because they will disappoint you, and you will disappoint them. There are NOT two groups:

1) the bad people and
2) the good people.

Instead, there are these two groups:

1) the bad people and
2) the bad people who have trusted in the forgiveness that Jesus offers through His death on the cross.

RELIGION ELEVATES PEOPLE

Religion elevates people, but people shouldn't be elevated. We should humble ourselves, not elevate ourselves.

I was watching the Catholic channel one day because I just find it interesting to listen to the ritual stuff. I saw a clip where a guy kissed the ring of the pope. The pope talked and got up and people paraded around him like he was a king. They basically worshipped him. But it's not just the pope that people worship, they also pray to the saints and they pray to Mary.

People are elevated, but they are all sinners just like you and me. They have all fallen short of the glory of God, just like you and me. Mary is a dead woman in heaven who doesn't hear our prayers, much less answer them. Saints and people have and do at times take the focus and the glory away from God, but it's not right.

Even the Son of Man came not to be served, but to serve. Jesus said,

> "Whoever would be great among you must be your servant, and whoever would be first among you must be slave of all. For even the Son of Man came not to be served but to serve, and to give his life as a ransom for many."

Jesus is God and Jesus is supposed to be worshipped. But Jesus makes the point that true greatness is found in humility, not in self-exaltation. This is why Jesus washed the disciples' feet. Jesus humbled Himself and became obedient to death, even death on a cross. But we love the gold and the robes and the incense and the show. It looks extravagant and special ... and it smells religious, but Jesus doesn't like it.

I was working at a swimming pool and spa company one summer. I only wanted to get a paycheck and I had no passion for pools and spas. I couldn't even afford one. I just got the job to make the money. Though I dreaded doing the job, I still worked hard.

I felt like complaining one day as I walked by the bathroom next to the warehouse. I noticed a guy on his knees in the bathroom cleaning the toilet. Then I saw who it was. It was the owner of the company, an owner of a pool and spa company who ships all over the country was on his hands and knees scrubbing the toilet. He had employees to do that, but he was doing it.

That example changed the way I viewed working for him. When he wanted something done, I worked my tail off for him. I respected him, and I still respect him to this day.

That's how Jesus was. The owner of the universe, the creator of mankind ... born in a stable and washing the feet of His followers. Jesus was a servant, which is a little different than kissing a ring, wearing a long robe, and burning incense.

THE HEART OF THE ISSUE

Religion focuses on issues, but Christ focuses on the heart. I've heard people say that they can't come to church because they don't listen to Christian music or they watch R-rated movies or they smoke.

Religion is focused on all of these issues, but we as Christians should be focused on the person, on the heart.

We must love and reach people and understand that God will impact their heart and begin to grow the areas of their lives that need to be changed. It's not our job to make them change everything externally. Instead, it's our job to expose them to the Savior who will produce change from the inside out!

Do we really love the community? Do we really love people who don't know Jesus? One day I was talking with a guy in the alley behind my old apartment. He didn't know I was a pastor. It was a great conversation. He was talking about himself, about his life, his family, and his work. He was cursing and laughing and just being himself. I got to see him for who he really was.

Then he asked, "So what do you do?"

I told him I was a pastor, then he got a little quiet. Then he said something like, "Well, I go to church every once in a while" and "I'm trying to be a good person." He also didn't curse for the rest of the conversation.

This guy, standing behind my old apartment, said something that really stuck with me. He said, "You know what gets me with Christians?"

> **Love OTHeRS SiMPLY BeCaUSe Jesus LOVeS YOU. THeRe iS NO eND TO THaT COMMaND.**

I said, "What?"

He then told me that he knew some Christians who would tell him that they loved him, they would invite him into their home, they would call him and text him and act like they really cared about him ... but after a period of time they cut him off because he didn't convert.

Is that what we are supposed to do? Love people with an agenda to convert them and if they don't come to faith in Jesus, then cut them off and don't talk to them anymore?

I felt for this guy. In his mind they said they loved him but their love was conditional to his conversion and when it didn't happen in what they would consider a reasonable time period they cut him off completely.

JESUS LOVED JUDAS

I began to think about Jesus and Judas. We don't operate like Jesus did. Have you ever thought about the way Jesus treated Judas. Jesus knew He came to die and He knew that Judas was going to betray Him. So here is Jesus, knowing for the entire three years He walked with Judas that Judas was going to betray Him, yet He doesn't quit loving Judas.

I imagine all of the nights that Jesus walked with Judas, ate with Judas, sat on the hillside and had a drink with Judas. Jesus just invested into the life of Judas, and the whole time Jesus knew that Judas was going to betray Him.

I began to ask myself, "Do I have that type of love? Would I love people even if they never converted? Would I love people if I knew they were going to betray me and walk away?"

Jesus poured into and loved a man whom He knew was going to betray Him and leave Him. I think that gives us incredible insight into the way we are supposed to love.

We are to love and love and love regardless of what the response is because as followers of Jesus it's what we do and it's who we are. We don't love for a certain response. We love because Jesus loves us and we are His kids and it's who we are and it's what we do and it fills us with joy to love people regardless of how they respond to us.

LOVE YOUR ENEMIES

Jesus said,

> "You have heard that it was said, 'You shall love your neighbor and hate your enemy.' But I say to you, Love your enemies and pray for those who persecute you, so that you may be sons of your Father who is in heaven.
>
> For He makes His sun rise on the evil and on the good, and sends rain on the just and on the unjust.

For if you love those who love you, what reward do you have? Do not even the tax collectors do the same? And if you greet only your brothers, what more are you doing than others? Do not even the Gentiles do the same?"

Don't just love the Christians in the church, but step outside of your comfort zone, pop your bubble, and love the people who are mean to you, who have bad attitudes, who let their dog take a dump on your lawn, or who blast their music too loud. Love them, get to know them, take an interest in them, and invest in them in whatever way possible.

IF YOU WANT TO LOVE PEOPLE, YOU HAVE TO GET PAST YOUR NEED FOR THEM TO LIKE YOU.

People are not going to come to Jesus, have their lives changed, and find fulfillment because you say your prayers or listen to Christian radio or sport a new bumper sticker. People are going to be impacted because you love them when they are hard to love.

A key concept that has really made a difference in my love for people is this: "If you want to love people, you have to get past your need for them to like you."

Again, "If you want to love people, you have to get past your need for them to like you." Let that soak in a bit.

Love them and love them and love them and love them and don't worry about them liking you back. It doesn't matter if they do or not. You are just going to love them. You aren't looking for a response. You are already happy and fulfilled in your relationship with God.

If you don't need them to like you back or for them to respond to you positively or for them to convert, then you can really love them with no strings attached. You just show love and compassion and care.

LOVE IS A CHOICE

What about people who have bad-mouthed you or your family for years? You have to understand love is a choice. You will choose to treat them in a loving way, pray for them, and care about their eternal soul. I am not saying you need to have an emotional connection with your enemies. You will not feel gooey love toward your enemies, nor will you be oozing with affection and emotional drive. It will drive you nuts to love them, but do it anyway.

See them as sinners for whom Jesus died. Choose to love them in spite of what they have done toward you or others.

It is incredibly freeing when you choose to love. Understand that you may never particularly care for them, but you still choose to love them. You still pray for them.

We used to take our youth group to a music festival called *Creation*, which had some of the biggest Christian bands in the country. It was an awesome opportunity to get away with the youth, and the youth often brought along a lot of their friends who were not Christians. It was great.

The conversations were engaging and my favorite part of the week was the chats out at the bonfire late at night as we'd eat smores and talk about God. It was this event that many parents would call me about, asking if certain "bad kids" were going to be there. They didn't want their kids being negatively influenced by the "bad kids." It was a shame because these parents had no idea what the parents of the "bad kids" were saying.

I HAVE TO KEEP MY KIDS AWAY FROM THE BAD KIDS, RIGHT?

Some parents of the "bad kids" would also call. They were so excited that their kids were going to *Creation* and they would tell me that they really hoped their kids would make connections with the "good kids" because they wanted the "good kids" to positively affect their children. They wanted their child, one of the "bad kids," to be around Christian kids and to develop a relationship with God.

But the parents of the "good kids" had no idea that the parents of the "bad kids" were praying for the kids to make a connection. Instead, the parents of the "good kids" were trying to keep the kids separated. (And by the way, in my experience, the "good kids" are often the ones who simply do a better job of hiding things from their parents and are sometimes just as bad, if not worse, than the "bad kids.") So, your kids are probably not completely innocent either ... seriously.

CHAPTER 9

Empty Rituals

Jesus is concerned with your heart, not your empty rituals.

Matt 15:18-20 says it well:

> "But what comes out of the mouth proceeds form the heart, and this defiles a person. For out of the heart come evil thoughts, murder, adultery, sexual immorality, theft, false witness, slander. These are what defile a person. But to eat with unwashed hands does not defile anyone."

Ritualism and hand washing was not what God wanted from them. Jesus noticed they obeyed their own self-imposed rules, but they were not right with God from the heart!

It's really not that important what version of the Bible you are using ... it's more important that you deal with your addiction to porn that is ruining your view of women and is ultimately going to affect your sex life when you are married. And if you are married, it's even worse.

Go ahead and wear shorts or wear a suit, it really doesn't matter, but stop flirting with the woman you are working with because you don't feel like you are getting enough attention from your wife at home. It's going to ruin your marriage and your family and rot you from the inside out.

So the ritualistic stuff is not so significant. The heart and the deeper issues that impact the way we live, those are what God wants to grab ahold of.

PRAYER WITH MEANING
It's a challenge for many to determine what is meaningful prayer and what is ritualistic prayer.

Matt 6:5-13 explains:

> "And when you pray, you must not be like the hypocrites. For they love to stand and pray in the synagogues and at the street corners, that they may be seen by others. Truly, I say to you, they have received their reward.
>
> But when you pray, go into your room and shut the door and pray to your Father who is in secret. And your Father who sees in secret will reward you. And when you pray, do not heap up empty phrases as the Gentiles do, for they think that they will be heard for their many words.
>
> Do not be like them, for your father knows what you need before you ask him. Pray then like this: Our father in heaven, hallowed be your name. Your kingdom come, your will be done, on earth as it is in heaven. Give us this day our daily bread, and forgive us our debts, as we also have forgiven our debtors. And lead us not into temptation but deliver us from evil."

Jesus really cuts down to the heart of it all. Religious people might be noticed, but that doesn't in any way mean that God is pleased with them or that they are at a good place spiritually speaking.

Pretty much all they get out of it is that people think they look really good. People look up to them. The religious are the ones who love for others to know they are big givers. They love to show off how many Bible verses they have memorized and they like to talk about how they want to get "deeper" spiritually.

Jesus DOeSN'T WaNT US TO SPOUT OFF MeaNiNGLeSS, MeMORiZeD PRaYeRS.

Jesus' point was that when we give, we don't even let the left hand know what the right hand is doing. We go out of our way for people to NOT see how religious we are.

MY FIRST SERMON

The first message I ever gave on a Sunday morning was from a section of Matthew 6 known as "The Lord's Prayer." The Senior Pastor was going to be away that Sunday and he asked me to speak, so I began studying the passage. What I found was a bit surprising to me.

After a lot of study and preparation, I was ready. I stood in front of the people that morning and I asked, "How many of you have the Lord's prayer memorized?" Pretty much everyone raised their hands. I began to say it with them.

As I dug into the message, I watched their eyebrows raise. I told them that the context of "The Lord's Prayer" was right after the religious people were praying in the synagogues and on the street corners so that other people would see them. These religious people would heap up empty phrases and use long memorized repetitious prayers, all for show. Jesus was saying, "Don't heap up empty phrases and don't do the memorized repetitious prayers. Instead, pray like this..." and he gave them a model.

The model Jesus gave listed the types of things to pray for, such as His kingdom to come, His will to be done, our daily bread, forgiveness of our sins, and deliverance from evil and temptation.

Here is the ironic part. Jesus tells us not to use these memorized prayers or to heap up these empty phrases like the Pharisees do, and then He gives us a model. The model was meant to help us not use meaningless repetition, but we turn around and memorize it. We memorize the very model that was meant to teach us NOT to memorize and recite empty word-for-word phrases.

We just don't get it! The point Jesus was making is that He wants us to be genuine and to pray for these types of important things, the things He listed in His prayer.

I finished the message that morning and afterwards I found out that the church used to recite "The Lord's prayer" every Sunday. Not surprisingly, some people definitely did not like what I had to say!

The message is always for someone else, right?

God is bothered by our empty repetition of the prayer He modeled for us. He's bothered by the fact that He doesn't have our hearts. He doesn't care about our religion, He wants us to love Him and want Him and desire Him and be real with Him. "God is great, God is good, let us thank Him for our food, Amen" with a fork in striking position is not what He's going for. He wants real communication, real passion, real love, and genuine conversation.

The actions of prayer and giving are good, but we must consider our hearts. I'm not saying that every person who prays "The Lord's Prayer" doesn't mean it. I'm also not saying that every person who dresses nice or gives a lot of money is a stuffy, self-righteous fake. I'm just saying that we need to consider our hearts and our appearances. Our religiosity means nothing to God, but our hearts mean everything.

SHOWING OFF

Again, the issue is the heart. Do you love Jesus or do you love people thinking you love Jesus and looking up to you and respecting you and loving you? Do you love others loving you and use the appearance of loving Jesus to get that? I'll repeat that again: Do you love others loving you and use the appearance of loving Jesus to get that? Because I think it's common, it's subtle, and maybe you say you aren't and you really are.

I'm not sure the guilty party ever really thinks it's them. The message is always perfect for somebody else, but if your true motive is a love for Jesus, then you don't care if anyone ever knows you are praying or learning or fasting or memorizing or meditating or giving. It doesn't matter. You aren't doing it for them. You are doing it just for Jesus. It's just you and Jesus' time and it's just as precious and amazing and refreshing, even more so, when no one knows but you and Jesus.

Mark 12:38-40 points out:

> "And in his teaching he said, "Beware of the scribes, who like to walk around in long robes and like greetings in the marketplaces and have the best seats in the synagogues and the places of honor at feasts, who devour widows' houses and for a pretense make long prayers. They will receive the greater condemnation."

Jesus spoke out against the scribes who walked around in long robes and liked greetings in the marketplaces and the best seats in the synagogues and the places of honor at feasts. These religious people dressed great. They looked superior. They even walked and talked like they were important. They didn't get paid for their services, so they depended on the hospitality of really dedicated Jews ... and some of them abused their position. They really were jerks. They would talk and pray in such a spiritual sounding way. Their lengthy prayers and "spiritualness" would get them trust and money.

They were like the televangelists urging people to send money so they can buy a jet plane and drive a Mercedes. Jesus tells us to watch out for these people. Beware. They look spiritual and they talk a big game, but they are in it for themselves. They don't have the slightest concern for hurting people around them. Instead, they use hurting people to pad their own wallets and to gain more prestige.

It's sick and pathetic. Ultimately God says He'll judge those who do this, and it won't be pretty.

SODOM'S APPLE

A few years ago I was visiting Israel. We went to a place called Ein Gedi, which is in the middle of the wilderness near the Dead Sea. There was a waterfall and caves, but before we went up to the waterfalls, the guide stopped us and showed us "Sodom's Apple."

Sodom's apple is a plant that looks so good, like you could pluck it and eat it right there in the middle of the desert, but if you pluck it and try to eat it, you will be in for a big surprise. The Sodom apple will dissolve in your hands, just like ashes.

It looked great on the outside but was empty and rotting on the inside. Maybe that's you, looking good on the outside, but rotting on the inside because you are trusting in your religion or in your appearance to make you right with God. Perhaps you have lost your love and passion for Jesus.

Jesus wants your heart, not your religion.

CHAPTER 10

Religion Steals God's Glory

When I was in Turkey, I visited the house where it was believed that Mary had lived. There were so many prayers written on paper and shoved into the wall that it looked like the wailing wall in Jerusalem ... even more packed. Prayers upon prayers upon prayers.

It was sad to see it because I think people genuinely believed those prayers to Mary would help them.

You can be sincere and be sincerely wrong. I've been in churches where there were statues of some of the disciples or of Mary or of angels. There were shrines to these individuals, dead people, who were at one time people like you and me. People literally bowed down and worshiped these images. They put money in front of them, they pray for their sins to be forgiven, or they pray for comfort, help, and deliverance.

He also told this parable to some who trusted in

But these dead people cannot provide forgiveness of sins or protect, help, deliver, or forgive anyone! They are dead.

In those religious exercises we steal the glory from God and give it to people, people who would be appalled and angry if they knew what we were doing in our religious churches.

IT'S ABOUT HIM, NOT US

Many times we walk out of church services and think about the music being just right (or just wrong), we think about ourselves, or we think about living a better life ... but God's name was never even mentioned.

We should never walk out of a church service thinking that its all about the good works we do or the image we give off to other people or the religious activities we take part in and forget about God completely. People are told to behave better or rewarded for their service or recognized for things they have done, but all the credit should be given to God, not us. How could we get it so wrong?

Religion ultimately begins to give glory to people. We like to take glory in our efforts, behavior, attendance, Bible version, and in our clothing. Or we like to give glory to our church, tradition, angels, mission work, or financial giving. We even take credit for not being one of the bad people, but where is God in all of this?

Luke 18:9-14 explains:

> He also told this parable to some who trusted in themselves that they were righteous, and treated others with contempt: "Two men went up into the temple to pray, one a Pharisee and the other a tax collector. The Pharisee, standing by himself, prayed thus: 'God, I thank you that I am not like other men, extortioners, unjust, adulterers, or even like this tax collector. I fast twice a week; I give tithes of all that I get.' But the tax collector, standing far off, would not even lift up his eyes to heaven, but beat his breast

saying, 'God, be merciful to me, a sinner!' I tell you, this man went down to his house justified, rather than the other. For everyone who exalts himself will be humbled, but the one who humbles himself will be exalted.

It's time to stop looking at each other and to start looking at God. The religious guy missed it completely. He trusted in himself and his own righteousness. But the truth is, our righteousness is because of Jesus standing in front of us, not because of ourselves. It's not about us. It's about God.

Some people thank God for working in their lives in incredible ways and that now their eyes are opened and they aren't "bad" like other people. The problem is that we are all bad, we are sinners, and we all fall short, just like other people.

> **RELIGION TRIES TO GIVE GOD'S GLORY TO PEOPLE.**

The focus is not on behavior, but on the God who forgives us in spite of us. It's time in church that we stop looking at each other and start looking at God. We've got to take our eyes off of us and put them on the only One who has the answers.

Psalm 106:19-22 states:

"They made a calf in Horeb and worshiped a metal image. They exchanged the glory of God for the image of an ox that eats grass. They forgot God, their Savior, who had done great things in Egypt, wondrous works in the land of Ham, and awesome deeds by the Red Sea."

SYMBOLS ARE NO HELP

Having a cross necklace or a statue or a verse above your door is not going to help you. I've even had people say that if we don't have a visible cross sitting in the worship center that we are not focusing on God.

If that is a requirement, then certainly that posed a problem for the early church that met outside on the hillsides, in each other's homes, on the grass, or on the floor. Even good symbols are just symbols. They will not change where we are at spiritually. They will not save us and they won't make us lucky. We need to consistently seek the God of the universe. When we take our eyes off of Him, we get all mixed up.

Relic worship will get you nothing in the end.

Those who trust in their relics and symbols will forget their relationship with the God who consistently works miraculously for them.

When I was in Rome, I saw all kinds of relics. I was told, "In this glass jar is a ring from the apostle Paul." It's a ring that one of God's sinful disciples wore, what's the big deal? But people would bow down to it and pray to it. They prayed to a ring. They literally communicated with a ring, but the ring did not respond (at least not verbally, not when I was there).

I've watched people kiss their cross necklaces and worship these relics like they will somehow do something for them! I'll kiss my cross necklace before I bat so that God can notice how spiritual I am and make my swing better and I'll hit more home runs.

Sadly behind much of the ritualism and relic worship is a belief that if you do these things and say these prayers then the results will come.

Colossians 2:18-23 says it pretty plainly:

> "Let no one disqualify you, insisting on asceticism and worship of angels, going on in detail about visions, puffed up without reason by his sensuous

mind, and not holding fast to the Head, from whom the whole body, nourished and knit together through its joints and ligaments, grows with a growth that is from God.

If with Christ you died to the elemental spirits of the world, why, as if you were still alive in the world, do you submit to regulations— Do not handle, do not taste, do not touch (referring to things that all perish as they are used)— according to human precepts and teachings?

These have indeed an appearance of wisdom in promoting self-made religion and asceticism and severity to the body, but they are of no value in stopping the indulgence of the flesh."

ARE WE SPIRITUALLY OBESE?

Christians like to sit around and be "deep." They love to dive into passages and tell stories about angels or discuss the end-times or debate free will and predestination or talk about their behavior and how they're trying to quit sinning (like it's a bad habit they're attempting to kick, like smoking).

And religious people are obsessed with saying "I want to be fed" or "I'm not going deep enough." Understand something: It's better that you learn and apply one thing than you learn 30 things and apply none.

So many Christians sit around and talk about their faith, but they aren't in love with Jesus. They sound smarter and they are more religious, but where is the passion for Jesus? They sit there and say, "Feed me, feed me, feed me," and they get spiritually obese.

It's a big problem in our churches today: spiritual obesity. Christians are constantly eating and there's no life change, no new passion for Jesus that results in a new life. And religious people just can't be fed enough and they are always complaining that they want more spiritual "meat."

It's not all about learning. Instead, what I learn should change who I am.

Religious people want to move past the gospel and talk about the "deep things," like premillenialism or amillenialism or covenant versus dispensational theology. They don't want to waste their time continuing to talk about the cross or about the gospel. In so doing, they are communicating a message that there is something "deeper" than the gospel, but there is not. There is nothing deeper or more amazing than Jesus on the cross for our sins.

WORSHIPING ANGELS

Many religious people like to worship angels. They talk about their guardian angels and they pray to their angel. They even have stories about the time when their guardian angel must have been there and protected them from something. Some talk more about angels than about God. And now there are TV shows and movies … let's face it, we are "touched" by angels.

We must recognize that if we pray to angels, we worship angels.

Revelation 19:9-10 says:

> "And the angel said to me, "Write this: blessed are those who are invited to the marriage supper of the lamb." And he said to me, "These are the true words of God." Then I fell down at his feet to worship him, but he said to me, "You must not do that! I am a fellow servant with you and your brothers who hold to the testimony of Jesus. Worship God."

The angel clearly and immediately made sure that he was not worshipped. "You must not do that … worship God!" Angels don't want our worship. Angels understand that all the worship, all the glory, and all the focus should go to God, not to them. As we pray to angels, we steal God's glory and give it to another one of His creations, the angels.

Angels are not bad. Angels are great, but they are created by God, they are not God, and they cannot forgive your sins or keep you safe. And when family members die, they don't become angels. They're people, and they don't turn into angels. And if your family members trusted in Jesus to take their place and remove the guilt of their sin, then they are in heaven and you'll see them again.

THE ANGEL SAID, "WORSHIP GOD!"

WORSHIPPING TRADITION

To worship is to give glory to, so if you worship tradition, you are giving glory to tradition, and that's not right.

Matt 15:6-9 explains:

> "So for the sake of your tradition you have made void the word of God. You hypocrites! Well did Isaiah prophesy of you when he said: This people honors me with their lips, but their heart is far from me; in vain do they worship me, teaching as doctrines the commandments of men."

It's all about your heart, not about tradition.

Jesus calls out the religious people for adding to God's commandments. Religious people have these special religious rules or laws that you aren't allowed to break. It's not what the Bible says, but it's what they teach.

According to the pharisaic tradition, priests washed their hands and feet prior to performing their duties. The pharisees jumped all over Jesus because His disciples weren't performing the ceremonial washings.

It still happens today. Religious people add to what the scripture really teaches. It is often motivated by preference. We really want something so we are going to teach that it's what God wants (remember the lighting preference, music style preference, clothing preference, etc.).

WHEN WE TOUCH PEOPLE, ARE THEY BETTER OR WORSE FOR IT?

Or religious people are worried that if we just teach what the Bible says that people will make bad choices, so they impose their personal guidelines or boundaries on others as if it's biblical truth.

The Bible doesn't say it's wrong to drink (it does say that drunkenness is sin), but the religious believe that if we think it's okay to drink that we'll then abuse it and get drunk. That's why drinking has been classified as wrong or sinful. They impose their boundary on others as if it's biblical truth, all the while not teaching the truth because they don't want us to abuse it.

But we can't add things to the Bible because it makes us comfortable. We have to speak as it says.

Religious people add their traditions to the Bible and then say, "We've always done it that way. You can't violate the tradition!"

I saw a calendar with a big picture of the running of the bulls in Spain. The caption underneath read, "Tradition — just because you've always done it that way doesn't mean it's not incredibly stupid."

STEALING GOD'S GLORY

I heard someone once say, "Trying to steal God's glory is like trying to extinguish the sun with an eye dropper. It's impossible. It's ridiculous. God's glory is so great that we can't steal it."

But in our pride we want the glory, we want the credit, and religion gives us that. Religion is the system that focuses on us and not on God. It attempts to put the glory back on religious people who are such wonderful "servants" of God.

Pride so easily creeps in and we start to believe the hype. We start to think highly of ourselves because of the things people tell us. As a result, we forget who gave us the very gifts we have. We forget where the blessings come from and we begin to feel really good about ourselves. Then we start to look down on those around us, as if they were inferior.

Remember that Satan's fall was the result of pride. Ezekiel explains it this way:

> "Your heart became proud because of your beauty; you corrupted your wisdom for the sake of your splendor. I cast you to the ground; I exposed you before kings, to feast their eyes on you. All who know you among the peoples are appalled at you; you have come to a dreadful end and shall be no more forever."

What a sad and pathetic end. The glory was no longer about God, it was about Satan, and Satan wanted the credit, the honor, and the recognition.

Confidence is not bad if it's in Jesus. I can do all things through Christ who strengthens me. When Jesus is behind it, it's possible, but we must always remember who the credit goes to ... because it isn't us.

1 Corinthians 3:18-23 says,

> "Let no one deceive himself. If anyone among you thinks that he is wise in this age, let him become a fool that he may become wise. For the wisdom of this world is folly with God. For it is written, 'He catches the wise in their craftiness,' and again, 'The Lord knows the thoughts of the wise, that they are futile.'

> *So let no one boast in men. For all things are yours,*
> *whether Paul or Apollos or Cephas or the world or*
> *life or death or the present or the future — all are*
> *yours, and you are Christ's and Christ is God's."*

Don't get a big head about being wise or about being a good Christian. Don't get strong on yourself, God gets the glory.

1 Corinthians 9:16 explains,

> *"For if I preach the gospel,that gives me no ground for*
> *boasting. For necessity is laid upon me. Woe to me if*
> *I do not preach the gospel!"*

ALL CREDIT GOES TO GOD

It's important that pastors understand that we can take absolutely no credit for anything good done in the ministry. It is all a result of God working in and through us all. We can, however, take credit for the bad, for slowing things down, and for messing things up.

We should do our absolute best and create a really good ministry, but any life change and saved souls are a result of God working in the hearts of people, not me and my hard work. We don't change people, only God does that, and when He does, we don't take the credit. God deserves the credit.

Galatians 6:14 states,

> *"But far be it from me to boast except in the cross of*
> *our Lord Jesus Christ, by which the world has been*
> *crucified to me, and I to the world."*

I'll never forget my favorite professor in college. He spoke to a large crowd and when he was finished, the crowd was so moved they started clapping and cheering. My professor looked into the crowd and said, "If you are cheering for God, continue, but if you are cheering for me, stop."

Ephesians 2:4-9 points out,

> "But God, being rich in mercy, because of the great
> love with which he loved us, even when we were dead
> in our trespasses, made us alive together with Christ-
> by grace you have been saved-and raised us up with
> him and seated us with him in the heavenly places in
> Christ Jesus, so that in the coming ages he might show
> the immeasurable riches of his grace in kindness
> toward us in Christ Jesus. For by grace you have been
> saved through faith. And this is not your own doing;
> it is the gift of God, not a result of works, so that no
> one may boast."

WE ARE DEAD WITHOUT GOD'S GIFT
Spiritually, we are dead, and religious ritualism doesn't save us.
Being good just won't happen. We are dead.

The key is that God is rich in mercy and pours His grace out on
people who totally don't deserve it. We would be so mistaken if
for a second we tried to take credit for the great change in our
lives, credit for our salvation, credit for being right with God, or
credit for having a future in heaven.
It's all a gift and it's all undeserved. While we are sinners, while
we are dead, while we are alienated from God, and while we
deserve punishment, He shows mercy to us.

Religion puts the focus back on me. It makes me think that if I
try harder, if I do more, then I'll be cool. But I can't ... only Jesus
can. Dead people can't help themselves. We are spiritually dead
and the only one who can bring us back to life is Jesus.

RELIGIOUS MANIPULATION
Several years ago, someone came into my office who wanted
things done in a more traditional and more religious manner. I
would not agree with his approach.

I try to be really up front with people and will not say "let me think about it" if I've already spent time thinking about it, I have an approach, I know what the vision is, and I know what the answer is. So when this guy told me what he wanted, I immediately said I wouldn't do it.

> Speak the Word, speak the truth, for that is enough.

He was appalled that I could say "no" to him, a man of considerable power and influence. When I rejected his request, he replied, "You do know I am one of the biggest financial contributors in the church, right?"

I said, "I don't care. I am not going to allow you to manipulate me with money. I have to make the decision I think God would want. It's not about what you want or what I want, God will provide the money."

THE DANGER OF RELIGIOUS RITUALISM

When Jesus gave the sermon on the mount, He gave blessings that describe Jesus' followers, and then He listed several woes to the religious people. This is a big deal. Jesus goes out of His way to preach a message to the religious people and call them out for their terrible sin.

The religious people have really created a big mess and Jesus exposed them for who they were and what they were doing. I think even though Jesus was so clear with the religious people, we miss the message of Jesus and turn His teaching and scripture into religious ritualism. I'm hoping we'll quit missing that and take Jesus at His word and see the dangers of the religious ritualism of the scribes and pharisees.

"You shut the kingdom of heaven in people's faces" — The first woe was that the teachers of the law and pharisees had actually taken people away from heaven and not toward it. People had begun to trust in their own works or performance. They had tried to stick to the religious system laid out by the pharisees and found it impossible to do.

The people were putting their trust in being right with God by their own efforts and they felt totally hopeless (and they really are hopeless). It's impossible for anyone to be right with God through their own perform-ance or "goodness," which is exactly why Jesus came. We can't do it. Jesus is our only hope.

To the Jews, the coming Messiah would be their only hope. Our hope is not in being good. Our hope is not Jesus plus being good. It's grace. It's God giving us what we don't deserve (through Jesus). If you add works to grace, then it's not grace any longer. You can't add anything to grace or it will fail to be grace.

> RELIGION PUTS THE FOCUS ON ME ... BUT IT'S SUPPOSED TO ONLY BE ABOUT Jesus.

If you add anything to what Jesus did on the cross, you don't understand the gospel, and if you don't understand the gospel, then you aren't right with God, and if you aren't right with God, then you can't go to heaven.

"You travel to make converts, then turn them into people like you ... even worse" — Jesus is calling them out because they would travel and spread their message and get people to follow them, but when these people followed them they would be given all these traditions and requirements to keep. Then the new believers would focus on trying to perform to the best of their abilities.

As a result, they began to turn into young pharisees who didn't truly understand grace or the gospel. Jesus told them that their converts were twice the children of hell as them. Their converts turned out to be like them, only worse. Jesus called them chil-dren of Gehenna. (Gehenna was a place where trash was burned.) Jesus was saying, "You get these people to follow you and they look like a burning pile of trash when you're done with them ... they are like you. You guys trust in altars and temples and gold and all that stuff and you miss the point!"

"Neglecting the most important issue of the law: Justice, mercy, and faithfulness" — The religious people actually tithed, but they neglected the more important issues of the law, like justice and mercy and faithfulness. Jesus actually says to them, "You strain out a gnat and swallow a camel." You are so meticulous to make sure that you follow through with the law or the commands that you are given, but you miss the point. You don't really love people. You don't really care about doing what's right. You don't really care about being faithful to God or others.

SPARKLING OUTSIDE, MOLDY INSIDE

Religious people clean the outside of the cup. The outside of the cup is sparkling and clean and looks great. The outside of the cup makes the religious look super-spiritual. They dress right, they talk right, and they look right, but inside they are filled with maggots and worms and they make Jesus sick. Inside they are full of greed and self-indulgence.

This is the religious. They are clean on the outside and looking great, but inside they are filled with dead men's bones, regret, shame, guilt, and fear.

Jesus points out that the pharisees justify themselves before men, but God knows their hearts. What is praised in front of men is sick and wicked in front of God. You can get all caught up in your religion and feel really good about it and other Christians can even praise you for being all religious, but what does God have to say about it?

You can share your religious experiences, post them on facebook or twitter, but God knows your heart. You can talk about loving God, but only God knows if you really love Him.

Most Christians talk about loving Jesus, but don't spend a whole lot of time with Him. They talk about prayer more than they really pray and they talk about reading scripture but don't spend much time actually diving into God's Word.

We all can look really good in front of other Christians, but where is our heart? God knows.

IS IT JUST JESUS?

As we've discussed, religion tries to steal God's glory. Religious people come into church and they feel that something is wrong because you aren't reciting The Lord's Prayer or they aren't kneeling or bowing or memorizing or quoting or singing a certain thing in a certain way.

When people don't perform these rituals, religion makes them feel like they aren't right with God. So they follow through with these rituals and they feel good, which further compounds the problem.

> Can it really be that easy? Is His grace really enough?

I've talked to countless people who said they loved the service and they were amazed at how awesome God was ... but they just felt like something was missing, like they weren't performing a duty or like they were supposed to do something that they hadn't done. It's as if they are thinking, "It couldn't be that easy. It can't be just grace. It can't be just Jesus ... I have to do something."

Religion says, "Look what I did." Instead, we should be saying, "Look what God did."

ARE YOU OKAY?

Religion tries to make me think that I'm okay and that I'm right with God ... when I'm not. And then I try to make myself good so that I'll be accepted.

Have you been on that treadmill?

The problem is that I constantly fall and live in guilt and shame, fully knowing how inadequate I am but afraid to admit it. I'm afraid because I have to keep up the image.

I'm tired of the religious style points (dressing the right way, talking the right talk, watching the right movies, and listening to the right music) that makes me look good but doesn't help me on the inside.

I'm tired of religion putting God in a box. I know, deep down inside, that there is more to God than what I experience at church. God is bigger than that!

I'm tired of religion saying that I need to avoid the "bad people." I know that I'm as bad as them; it's just that I'm dealing with different sins than they are.

I'm tired of religion saying that I need to pray to dead people or that I need to put my hope in an angel. I want to worship God and God alone.

I hate religion.

We should run from it.

Embrace, pursue, and love the Jesus who died on the cross in your place. He took your sins and through his Grace offers forgiveness and eternal hope. It's not about religious ritualism, it's about a relationship with Jesus Christ. He loved you so much He died in your place to eliminate your sin and pave the way for a relationship with you. He wants you, and you do nothing to make that happen. He made that happen ... religion didn't make that happen, the cross made that happen.

I love that.

ABOUT THE AUTHOR

Mike Jarrell received a Bible degree from Word of Life Bible Institute before obtaining a degree in Pastoral Ministries from Philadelphia Biblical University. Mike was a Youth Pastor for three years in the Philadelphia area before accepting the Lead Pastor position with Cornerstone Christian Church. He prefers to focus on his strongest abilities of teaching, sharing ideas, leadership-development, writing and setting vision for the church.

Mike started as Lead Pastor in February of 2007 when the church was just under 100 without a building. In just 4 years, under Mike's leadership, Cornerstone has grown from under 100 to over 600 in weekly attendance and continues to reach more in a very rural area. Mike is a part of K Club Team 500, which is a group of Pastors of churches of 500 or more in the Evangelical Free Denomination. He has been a guest speaker on different occasions. Mike leads a church that is effectively connecting with a younger unreached generation and is cutting edge in his approach to engaging the unreached.

Mike is thankful to have surrounded himself with a staff that he will tell you is more gifted in their areas than he is. Mike absolutely loves to have fun and believes Christians have unnecessary shame about having fun and take great pride in being extremely busy. Mike greatly values time with his family as a more important priority than his ministry.

www.ihatereligionbook.com